Praise for Ring-

"A good fun read ..."

— NINJA LIBRARIAN

"Claire Logan spins a tale that keeps you interested and wanting to read more."

— MY READING JOURNEYS

"All the characters are well developed, and the story is delightful."

— BARONESS BOOK TROVE

"... my favorite thing about this novel is the characters, especially Hector and Pamela. My second favorite is that the action is fast-paced, so you have have to be on your toes at times when trying to figure out the killer yourself."

— MELISSA WILLIAMS

"I recommend this book to cozy mystery readers that enjoy the look and feel and flavor of Prohibition Chicago."

— KAREN SIDDALL

To those of you taking second chances.

Ring-A-Ding Dead!

The Myriad Mysteries #1

Claire Logan

Copyright © 2019 Claire Logan

ISBN-13: 978-1-944223-32-8

Printed in the USA

All rights reserved.

This is a work of fiction. The story, all names, characters, and incidents portrayed in this production are fictitious. No identification with actual persons (living or deceased), buildings, events, locations, or products is intended or should be inferred.

1

When they first arrived in Chicago, the couple took a leisurely breakfast at a posh little cafe in the station, then spent an hour or so shopping for new, stylish clothes, suitable for their new city. While they were out, they had their hair cut and colored in the fashion of the day.

At first, the lady balked at displaying her ankles in public, not to mention bobbing her long hair. But afterward, she showed her new self to her new husband. "Mr. Jackson, how do I look?"

"Perfectly charming, my dear, as always."

As his tight-coiled hair was pressed and her thick curls dyed, she said, "We must decide what to do. Where shall we stay? What shall we do for a living? Shall we rent rooms? Or purchase an office?"

"Nonsense, my dear," Mr. Jackson said. "Everything has changed. After all that has happened, we deserve nothing but the very best."

When the hairdressers finished their work, the couple strolled out to the street, a porter carrying their purchases. Cars bustled past as the work day began.

Mr. Jackson flagged down a cab. "Myriad Hotel."

"Right away, sir." And off they went.

Mr. Jackson marveled at how quickly things could change. Yesterday he was a bachelor; just hours later, a husband.

As they rode, he watched his new wife. How fortunate he'd been to follow his instincts and offer her this marriage. How grateful he was that she'd accepted!

Mrs. Jackson peered out of the window, astonishment on her face. "The architecture is magnificent!"

Mr. Jackson felt surprised. "I didn't know you cared for such things."

"Oh, yes. I love it! Many of the buildings remind me of my home." She paused, eyes distant. "I wonder if they had the same architects." She leaned back on the cushioned seat. "What a wonderful place this is!"

The cabbie glanced quickly back. "First time here, then?"

"I've been here many a time," Mr. Jackson said. "But it's her first."

"What brings you here?"

"We're on our honeymoon," Mr. Jackson said.

The cabbie seemed touched. "Well, fine congrats to you both." He glanced at the lady. "You're gonna love it. Nice place, though it does get chilly in the winter. You arrived at the perfect time. And the nicest people you'll ever meet anywheres."

The exterior of Myriad Hotel was sumptuous: gray-white marble, trimmed in rosewood and brass. Yet no one greeted them out front, or stood to hold the door, as Mrs. Jackson had seen done at other hotels.

So the cab driver held the door for them, for which he got a good tip.

"Odd," Mr. Jackson said. "This hotel normally has such fine service."

Mrs. Jackson gaped at the lobby of Myriad Hotel: marble floors, rosewood paneling, Art Deco murals, and brass trimmings. In the center of the magnificent hall, an exquisitely carved fountain twice her height shot water past the second floor railings towards a glittering chandelier high on the vaulted ceiling. She turned to Mr. Jackson. "Oh, this is lovely!"

He beamed. "I so hoped you'd like it."

Yet for all its splendor, the lobby was empty.

The couple went across the wide hall to the front desk, a gleaming paneled affair, and rang the fine silvered bell.

No one answered.

So they stood there, waiting.

After a time, Mrs. Jackson called out. "Hello! Is anyone there?"

They waited a while more, but there was no answer.

"This is quite odd," Mr. Jackson said. "The last time I came here, the place was full at all hours of the day and night! Where could everyone be?" Mr. Jackson took her arm. "Come, my dear, let's sit."

Gratefully, she followed him to brass chairs cushioned in black velvet to rest herself, while Mr. Jackson (carrying their many packages) sat to her left.

Weariness washed over her. With everything that had happened over the past twenty-four hours, she hadn't slept — she couldn't.

A clock chimed ten. Good smells came from across the way, and from far off behind frosted doors of beveled glass, the sound of a dining room's chatter. But other than that, the place seemed deserted.

Mr. Jackson gestured at her right arm, which was in a sling. "How do you feel? Shall I find someone to help us?"

She patted his hand. "I've survived worse." She smiled at him. "Someone will be along soon. Let's just rest a while."

So they waited.

After a few moments, a stout woman with dark curls walked past. She wore a standard maid's uniform, black with a white apron and hat, and a white tag ringed in brass with dark lettering which read: Maria. "Have you been helped, sir?"

"Why, no," Mr. Jackson said. "We rang some time ago, but no one's answered."

The woman frowned towards the front desk. "That clerk has left his post again!"

She stormed over to a side door, then appeared at a doorway behind the counter. She looked down, then recoiled, eyes wide, letting out a startled scream.

Leaving their packages, the couple rushed to the desk, peering far over the counter.

Under the counter, a man lay there — dead.

2

At once, the lobby filled with people rushing around: maids, bellhops, busboys, and door men. The couple retreated to their seats to view the commotion.

Yet Mrs. Jackson felt disturbed. The man had been lying there, dead, the entire time!

After a while, police and coroner's men entered the lobby. These men, carrying black leather cases, strode towards the crowd milling around the front desk.

One, a stern older man in a cheap brown suit, focused on the couple. "You found the body?"

"The maid saw him first," Mr. Jackson said, "but we sat here for at least twenty minutes before that. We wanted to check in, but no one answered the bell."

The man gestured to a uniformed officer, who stationed himself at the end of the row of chairs. "Stay here until you're called." The man went to the door beside the front desk, disappearing behind it. Beyond that, the dining room's doors opened, confused guests pouring out. They stared at the scene, curiosity on their faces, before being waved past by uniformed men.

Mrs. Jackson had never seen anything like this in a hotel before. She turned to Mr. Jackson. "What do you think?"

"The man seemed quite uncommonly pale."

She had to agree: his face was much too pale, even for a dead man. And there was a familiar smell, one she couldn't quite place. Grief came from, it seemed, nowhere. She didn't even know the man! "The timing of this is distressing."

Mr. Jackson took her good hand in both of his. "My poor dear. I never wanted this to greet you on our arrival."

She clung to him, trying to put past memories of death behind her. There seemed to be nothing they could do but wait.

Men photographed the body, dusted for prints. Others marked and cordoned off the whole lobby this side of the magnificent marble fountain as the couple watched. Far past them, near the entrance, patrons milled about. Some stood in front of the gift shop staring across the lobby in their direction. A crowd peered through the beveled glass front windows behind them.

Mrs. Jackson felt exhausted. Her injured arm ached, tingled. She wanted nothing more than to lie down.

But first the police wanted to speak to them.

The stern-looking man brought the couple to a side room. A polished wooden table with four chairs sat in the center. "Never did see such goings-on here before," he snapped.

The man sounded annoyed with the whole affair!

He made a quick, dismissive gesture towards the chairs, so they sat. Then he sat across from them, opened a notepad, and frowned at them. "Sergeant Benjamin Nestor, Chicago Police. And you are?"

Mrs. Jackson didn't know whether to laugh at or be angry with his tone. But she stayed still, curious as to what bothered the man so.

Mr. Jackson extended his hand. "Hector and Pamela Jackson."

Sergeant Nestor ignored Mr. Jackson's hand, instead making notes on his pad with a jerking motion. "Your occupation?"

Mr. Jackson appeared unruffled by the man's sharp tone and angry demeanor. "I have lands and investments throughout the country. Well, to be honest, I have a small property overseas as well." He spoke of this wealth as if it were quite modest. He relaxed, leaning back. "I live off the income, and travel whenever the need arises."

Sergeant Nestor's jaw tightened, and he scratched on his notepad. "Your business here?"

"We've only just arrived," Mr. Jackson said, as if having embarked upon a grand adventure. "We're on our honeymoon."

The sergeant's face turned sour, cynical. "Congratulations." Then he frowned. "Tell me what you saw."

They recounted the little they did see: an extremely pale, dark-haired man lying dead, a bone-dry teacup and saucer on the floor beside him. "It did seem odd," Mrs. Jackson said (when asked), "that the door-men were absent."

"That is odd." Sergeant Nestor seemed to honestly consider the matter.

Mrs. Jackson had the sergeant pegged: uncomfortable with those above his station. A perennial chip on a pugnacious shoulder. A man who preferred being in control.

He probably hated being called to such an opulent hotel.

The sergeant frowned at her sling as if it offended him. "What happened there?"

She decided simple candor was the best option. "I had surgery."

"Before your wedding?"

"It was somewhat of an emergency." She shrugged, unsure how much more to say. "It couldn't be helped."

He scowled at this, but apparently could find nothing more to ask.

Mr. Jackson gave her a quick glance. "We both have experience as private investigators. If you —"

"Both?" The officer seemed dubious.

"Why certainly," Mr. Jackson said. "I've only ever been an amateur. But my wife was a professional investigator for some time. Before our marriage, of course." He turned to her with a fond smile, and she nodded. "You might say that's how we came to know each other."

Mrs. Jackson felt amused, both by Mr. Jackson's words and the sergeant's expression. "Do you not have woman detectives here?"

"Well, uh ... of course!" Sergeant Nestor glanced between the couple as if at a loss. Then he frowned, straightening. "Certainly."

Mr. Jackson said, "I'm sure you have your own people for such things, but if we can be of any assistance —"

A hint of sarcasm laced the man's tone. "I'll be sure to ask." The sergeant rose, handed Mr. Jackson his card. "If you remember anything else, call."

After the sergeant left, a young uniformed officer poked his head in. "Wait here." He pulled the door shut.

The couple glanced at each other and shrugged.

Mrs. Jackson said, "Call?"

"This place is a marvel. It has telephones in every room!"

"Telephones in every room?" She shook her head, astonished. "A far cry from home, I must say."

"Indeed it is."

***

Mr. Jackson surveyed his wife. She looked pale, with dark circles under her eyes. He needed to get her to their rooms.

He wasn't used to this. All his life, he went where he pleased, when he wanted, and it'd been rare that another person was dependent upon him.

But the situation was out of his control. These police would take anything which caused a break from their protocol as suspicious, and the last thing they needed right now was to fall under suspicion.

A few moments later, the manager came in. He offered credit to their account for a full week's stay, which seemed quite generous. "Do you need anything else? Anything at all."

"Your best two-bedroom suite," Mr. Jackson said. "Money is no object. And my wife needs a lady's maid. Preferably one with experience in caring for wounds."

The manager glanced at her arm in its sling. "I'll send for one right away."

"You're too kind," Mr. Jackson said.

"And will you be needing a valet, sir? To assist you in dressing."

This was the first time staying in Chicago that he'd been offered one. "Why, if one is available, of course."

"Most certainly, sir. Never fear, we only use the finest procurement services. You may hire by the day, hour, or week."

"We'll be here at least a week," Mr. Jackson said, amused. "But I'll meet the fellow first."

"Of course, sir." the manager said, and began to rise. "Now, if you'll —"

To Mr. Jackson's surprise, his wife said, "A question, if you please, sir."

The manager blinked. "Why, of course."

"Was your clerk scheduled to work today?"

"No," the manager said, and he also seemed surprised. "Certainly not. I'll have to look into it, but it seems another fellow switched with him for this morning without notifying me. He'll get a stern talking-to."

"The poor man," Mr. Jackson said. "To help a fellow out, then die? A pity."

"Indeed it was," the manager said, but he didn't sound sincere. "Now, if you'll return to the lobby, I'll have someone show you to your rooms shortly."

By the time the couple stepped into the hallway, the body of the young man had been carried away.

Yet the lobby was full of commotion. A dark wooden rectangular folding table laden with many paper bags and one pale yellow folder had been set up off to one side. Sergeant Nestor stood behind the table, conversing with a man in a similar suit.

Uniformed men moved back and forth between the table and the front desk. Some carried baskets filled with sealed brown paper sacks, which they placed on the table. Others carried documents, which they placed in the folder. Still other men stood, clipboards in hand, making notes and flipping pages.

Shades had been pulled over the windows against the late morning sun, which streamed in through the glass front entryway.

To Mr. Jackson's relief, reporters were being kept outside by uniformed police. He moved his wife and their packages to a seat well away from the doors.

They hadn't slept the entire trip, and his wife must be weary. She'd made no complaint about her injury, but it worried him just the same. He put his arm around her. "Rest your head on my shoulder." To his surprise, she did so without protest, but her eyes stayed open.

The trip to their suite was a noisy affair. Maids and bellboys followed them with questions all the way to the elevator.

Mr. Jackson turned to face them. "My dear people. We've had a long, tiring journey. Might we discuss this another time?"

"Of course, sir," they mumbled, moving away.

The bellboy pushing the cart with their packages clearly wanted to ask more but fortunately stayed quiet. For that, Mr. Jackson gave the man a good tip.

Their suite was on the thirty-second floor, and the rooms were even finer than he remembered. Two bedrooms, freshly painted, with new bed-covers. They had separate baths and a generous parlor with its own door to the hallway. The rooms held fruit, flowers, a stunning view of the lake, and every amenity one might hope for.

Once the door closed, his wife sagged onto a bed. "At last."

He sat, wrapped his arms around her, lay her head on his shoulder. Kissed her forehead with a tenderness which surprised himself. "We'll be safe here. We can finally rest."

3

A t first, all Mrs. Jackson wanted was to sleep. But alas, it was not to be: the lady's maid, a Mrs. Octavia Knight, arrived soon after. Mr. Jackson had retired to the other bedroom with his packages, leaving her to deal with the woman.

However, when she stood, she found that she felt refreshed. So she interviewed the woman, who was perhaps forty, at a small table of polished rosewood which lay near the window. "How long have you been a lady's maid?"

Mrs. Knight smiled to herself. "A little over a year. But before that I was nurse to one of the great families. Been taking care of injury all my life. Don't suppose you'd know any of them, being from out of town as you are."

Mrs. Jackson felt a bit embarrassed. "Is it that obvious?"

"Your accent." Mrs. Knight stopped, face puzzled, then continued. "But their children are grown and gone.

The older ones are down at the heels, so I was let go." She let out a regretful sigh. "It caused some trouble with the finances at first as my husband's ill. I'm busy enough now with this temporary work. I've come to meet many a fine family this way."

Mrs. Jackson felt impressed. "It sounds quite an adventure."

"It has been, ma'am."

"Will your husband's illness cause problems with your schedule?"

"Oh, no, ma'am. He was injured in the war, then he had that horrible flu, then pneumonia after. He still doesn't breathe well. He can't work much, but he can take care of himself just fine."

This woman seemed competent enough. "I'll need you to help with my bath, and dress me for breakfast and dinner," Mrs. Jackson pointed to the sling, "so long as I have this on."

"Yes, ma'am. And I'll put away your packages. Would you like a bath? The manager said you'd just arrived."

"That would be wonderful."

The bathing room was large, decorated in black and white tile with brass trimmings. The tub was white porcelain, legs and all. The fittings for the sink and tub were brass, and the tub had three black ceramic handles.

Mrs. Knight took off Mrs. Jackson's sling and put it to soak in the sink. The maid tsk'd and shook her head at the large, newly sutured wound in the bend of Mrs. Jackson's right elbow. But she never asked about it, for which Mrs. Jackson felt most grateful.

Mrs. Knight said, "What good fortune that you've chosen this place!" She pointed at the center tap. "The Myriad has mineral spring water piped in — just lovely for healing wounds and all sorts of sickness."

"Is that so?"

"Yes! People come from all over the world just to bathe downstairs at the spa!"

Could this be the reason that Mr. Jackson chose this hotel? If so, it was certainly quick thinking! And it showed a care for her welfare that she found touching.

If I only would have known, she thought, remembering their bitter battles in the past.

She felt an instant's hesitation to be undressed by a stranger. And in all the commotion, she'd completely forgotten about the gun in its holster just below her right knee until the maid saw it, eyes wide.

Mrs. Jackson felt amused at Mrs. Knight's expression. "There's no need to touch the gun. Unbuckle the holster from my leg, if you will, and place it on the dresser."

To her surprise and relief, the maid never asked why she had it.

It felt wonderful to soak in the hot water while her sling was being washed and dried. But the injection the surgeon had given her was wearing off, and her arm began to hurt in earnest.

Mrs. Knight gently patted the wound dry and applied an ointment, wrapping it with the bandages she'd brought with her. "Changing this once or twice daily should do just fine." She slipped a cotton day dress over Mrs. Jackson's head, then measured out a dose of pain medication. "That sling will be a while drying. Do you need help putting it on?"

"Mr. Jackson can do that if needed."

"Very good, ma'am." She glanced around, then took a wide-toothed comb from her bag. "Come into the other room and I'll comb out your hair."

While the maid dried and combed her hair, Mrs. Jackson surveyed her bound arm. She'd had little experience in such things, but the bandaging seemed at least as professionally done as when applied by the surgeon's nurse the night before. "I'm glad to have you, Mrs. Knight — you've done fine work."

The maid curtsied. "Thank you." She began to collect her things. "I'll be back at seven to dress you for dinner."

Whether from the medication or the bath, Mrs. Jackson felt quite sleepy. "No need: we'll be staying in. Perhaps tomorrow morning at nine?"

"Yes, ma'am. I'll see you then. Rest well."

Once the maid left, Mrs. Jackson put her holster and gun in the top drawer of the dresser, placed a shawl atop it, then lay in bed with her day dress still on.

***

While Mrs. Jackson was being attended to, Mr. Jackson went to his room on the far side of the parlor and set down his packages by the wall.

Collapsing into a chair, he surveyed the room. Everything had changed since the last time he'd been here. And the last twelve hours had gone differently than he could have possibly imagined.

A few moments later, his manservant arrived, a Mr. Norman Vienna. Brown hair and eyes, pale skin. A well-cut black silk suit.

Quite the looker, indeed.

"Good morning, sir," Mr. Vienna said. "May I enter?"

Mr. Jackson felt a bit flustered, and berated himself. *None of that here, not now.* "Yes, please, do come in." He gestured towards the room, and the man came past. "I presume you're sent by the management?"

"Yes, sir. I work for the Howell-Green procurement agency, contracted by the hotel. You pay the hotel for my services once I send them the bill."

He seemed quite young. "How long have you done this work, if I may ask?"

"Several years now, sir. I began as valet to a young man who died of malaria while on vacation." His gaze fell. "He was much loved. His death broke the family, sad to say. I was let go when the property was sold."

"How dreadful!"

Mr. Vienna shook his head, not meeting Mr. Jackson's eye. "It was, sir. The young master was only seventeen. He never would have wanted things to end so." Then he straightened. "After that, I served as valet to a medical officer in the war. I have excellent references, sir, and will do you well for as long as you stay here."

Mr. Jackson felt touched by the man's tale. "I don't have much here." He pointed at the packages along the wall. "But I'll require you before breakfast and dinner, for a dress and a shave. And perhaps a trim here and there."

At the last, the man raised an eyebrow. "How long do you plan to stay, then, sir?"

"Our plans are open at present." He gave a quick glance at the closed door leading to his wife's bedroom.

"How many are in your party, sir? If I may ask."

"Just my wife and I. She's speaking with her maid now."

"Very good, sir. I'll put away your things then, if we're done here."

Mr. Jackson sat watching the young man work with a sense of loss. So much death.

Why did the clerk downstairs die? Could it have been natural for such a young man to fall dead on the job?

Something about it felt wrong.

After Mr. Vienna left, Mr. Jackson knocked softly at his wife's door. Hearing no answer, he peeked in.

She lay upon her bed, eyes closed, black curls spread across her pillow.

He pulled the covers over her shoulder, feeling a surprising fondness for her. He kissed her forehead, then returned to his rooms to lie down, falling asleep at once.

A small noise woke him.

His wife peered in through the door to her room. "I'm sorry to bother you." She looked abashed. "But I need your help."

It took him a moment to remember where he was. "I'll be in momentarily." He pulled on his trousers and a shirt, then went into his wife's room.

She stood in the middle of the room fumbling with her sling. The late afternoon sun streamed golden onto the floor. "I can't seem to manage the straps."

For a moment, he sat on the back of a chair, trying to make sense of the task at hand. Adjusting the straps, he fit the sling to her arm.

Their eyes met, and she turned away. "Thanks." She took an apple from the bowl on the dresser. "Did your manservant arrive yet?"

"He did! Ever so congenial fellow. Not that I have a great many things with me, but it'll be nice to have someone else fuss over them."

"And they call them valets here."

"Indeed. And the men who bring the cars, too, although you must never confuse them." He laughed at the thought. "To ask a personal manservant to fetch your car would be most offensive, and vice versa."

"I suppose never leaving my town makes me quite unaware of the world beyond." She sat at the table by the window.

He remembered the first time he'd traveled. This place must be quite different than what she was used to.

"Do you think we might be able to travel more? Once I'm well, of course."

He slumped into the chair across from her. "We can go anywhere you wish."

"How long do you think we should stay here?"

He shrugged. "We have a week's credit. But we can stay as long as you like."

Fear touched her eyes. "It's just ... I don't like all the police about."

"Let's stay in our rooms tonight. I'll call room service for dinner." He'd more than half expected to find her gone when he woke. A change, but a fortunate one. "We've given our statements, so they should have no further use for us." He grinned. "Just the way I like it."

She smiled to herself at that last bit. "You made it sound that you were a busy man. Do you not have a schedule?"

He stretched back, hands behind his head. "I'm on my honeymoon, don't you know?" He gave her a wink and a smile. "Unless some disaster occurs, I don't need to be anywhere." He chuckled. "Perhaps not even then. I have men in every city, capable of handling most situations." Which was fortunate, as none of them knew where he was at present.

"I never realized." She sounded both awed and impressed. "Perhaps someday I'll have a retinue of my own." She raised her injured arm with a wry smile. "If I survive this."

A knock came at the parlor door.

Mr. Jackson struggled to his feet. "Whoever could that be?" He turned to his wife. "I'll take care of this."

He left his wife's room, closing the door behind him, then tucked in his shirt and answered.

To his surprise, the manager stood there. "May I come in?"

"Is something wrong?"

"Why, no — not at all. I'm ever so sorry to intrude. But I need to speak with you most urgently."

What could this possibly be about? He opened the door wide. "Of course. Come in."

Their parlor had a long sofa by the windows, with a coffee table and overstuffed chairs. But there was also a large round rosewood table off to the side with several straight-backed chairs around it. Mr. Jackson gestured to one. "Please, sit down."

They went to the table, sat.

"I hope you're both well," the manager said.

"We are. Thank you." This situation was unlike anything he'd experienced here before. "How may I help?"

The manager, who had been looking out of the window, hesitated.

Mr. Jackson felt weary. "You said the matter was urgent?"

"Well —" the manager seemed embarrassed. "I listened at the door when you spoke with the police." Then he leaned forward. "You said you'd been private investigators ..."

Mr. Jackson peered at him, trying to understand. "Are you offering us a **job**?"

"I know you're on your honeymoon. I get it." He shifted, glanced around. "But the man who owns this hotel wants answers, and —" his face paled. "Let's just say he's not the sort of man you want to make angry."

Mr. Jackson nodded sagely. "We do have some small experience with that sort."

"Anything you can learn — anything at all — we'd be grateful. Most grateful."

Interesting, Mr. Jackson thought. If this owner was the sort of man he sounded like, this might be an opportunity. "I have permission to speak with your staff, then?"

Relief crossed the manager's face. "Of course! Any time. Whatever you need is yours."

After the manager left, Mr. Jackson went back to his wife's room. "You're not going to believe this."

"What did he want?"

"He wants us to poke around, talk with the staff — by order of the hotel's owner. Who apparently isn't someone you make unhappy."

His wife's face turned amused. "Ah. So things are not so different here after all."

4

No one knew where the couple had come from.

They didn't order lunch. Which was understandable, given that they had just witnessed death. But they didn't order tea or supper either. The waitstaff fidgeted: were the couple well?

"Good grief," the manager said, clearly annoyed at the crew. "They're on their honeymoon. What do you imagine they're doing? Go on, now, get to work!"

But many in the staff let out a sigh of relief when the couple ordered a late dinner in their rooms.

When the bellhop returned from serving them, the others clamored around him. Surely there was something, anything they could learn about the couple who found the body of their co-worker. Something that might tell them how or why he died.

But the bellhop had little to tell. "The gent answered: said the missus was a-sleeping. Tipped well, he did."

So after a while the staff returned to their duties, wary, disturbed, and some, afraid.

***

Mr. Jackson lay in his room late at night, his door to the parlor open, the lamp on, gazing at the ceiling, not really thinking of anything. And yet he heard a soft weeping.

He crept to his wife's door, opened it softly. His wife lay curled on her left side, facing him, her face awash with tears.

"I'm sorry," she sobbed.

"No," he said. "Don't be. Is it your arm?"

She shook her head and wept harder.

He knelt before her, moving wet curls from her face. He kissed her forehead gently, marveling that she of all people felt safe to cry near him. "It feels unbearable."

She nodded. Her body shook with sobbing, yet after a time, she seemed more at peace, her eyes far away. "How did you bear it?"

He let himself collapse upon the floor to gaze upon her face, and spoke in utter honesty. "I don't know. I suppose you just do."

Her hand came from under the sheets to grasp his. "Don't leave me."

It broke his heart. He climbed into bed beside her, lying on top of the covers, and held her as if she were a small girl. He had a sharp, poignant memory of his little sister climbing into his bed late at night, back in the days of childhood.

His sister was now prosperous, grown and married, with children of her own, who were very likely crawling into bed beside her now. That thought made him smile.

But he missed her. And under the circumstances, it was doubtful he'd ever see her again. "I'll never leave you." He held his wife close, listening to the quiet sounds of the room. "I promise. I'll never leave you, no matter what."

***

The pair did come down for breakfast the next day, and the staff all agreed that they looked impressive. The gentleman — for clearly he was a gentleman, by his manners and dress — was all a fine gentleman should be. Tall, past thirty, quite dark-skinned, and very handsome.

The lady was a few years younger. Slender, with light brown skin and blue eyes, she was fashionably yet modestly dressed, as befitted a respectable woman of means, a cute little cloche hat atop thick black curls. Her right arm was in a sling, and she didn't speak much. Perhaps her injury pained her.

The vast dining room was filled with large round tables, which the guests sat around.

A waiter approached. Young, slender, brown hair and eyes. His face, an even tan. The tag on his shirt read:

George. He said to Mr. Jackson, "What can I get you, sir?"

"Coffee, heavy cream, no sugar," Mr. Jackson said. "Make it about your color."

"Right away, sir."

The Myriad Hotel's most illustrious guest, the dowager Duchess Cordelia Stayman, had come to breakfast with her husband Albert in a silk morning dress, with a beaded hat and robe. "Horrid business," she said, as the waiter served her. "Imagine, such a young man simply dropping dead!"

Mrs. Jackson went pale, her eyes red.

"Now, Cordelia," Albert said. "You'll spoil breakfast."

Mr. Jackson turned to his wife. "Are you well?"

She dabbed her eyes. "I agree. It's horrid."

Mr. Jackson put a glass of water into his wife's left hand. "Here. Drink something. You'll feel better."

So she did, but it seemed an effort for her to smile.

"I'm sorry, my dear," the dowager said. "My old mouth runs away with me." She turned towards the large frosted-glass doors. Past them, the clear light of a sunny late morning streamed onto the lobby floor. "What a lovely day it is."

Having served drinks, the staff began to serve the breakfasts.

"It is lovely," Mrs. Jackson said after a moment. She turned to her husband. "Perhaps after breakfast, we might take a stroll?"

"That would be splendid," Mr. Jackson said. "And we must see all the sights."

"Oh, yes," the dowager said. "There's so much to do here! There's a park right nearby. And the weather is lovely this time of year. Is this your first visit?"

"Her first," Mr. Jackson said.

"How long are you here for?"

Mr. Jackson said, "Our plans are open as yet."

"Marvelous." She turned to Mrs. Jackson. "We must plan out your stay here, so you don't miss a thing!"

"Cordelia," Albert said. "Surely these people can plan out their own stay."

She laughed, but her cheeks colored. "I'm sorry — I just get so excited to show everything. It isn't often you get the opportunity to share such a fine city."

A pretty young blonde woman came by carrying a tray. Her name-tag read: Agnes. "Cigars? Cigarettes?"

"I'll take some," Mrs. Jackson said. "And matches, if you have them.

"No, thank you," Mr. Jackson said at the same time. He turned to the dowager. "What brings you to Chicago?"

"Oh, we've lived here at the hotel these three years," Albert said. "Quite economical. Everything you need, and no servants or lands to manage." He turned to his wife. "Remember how much bother we had?"

The dowager, in the midst of drinking her tea, stopped with a grimace, then nodded. "Terrible expense."

Mrs. Jackson put the cigarettes and matches in her pocket and said, "Living at a hotel? I'd never considered such a thing!"

"It's ever so fashionable," the lady sitting to Mrs. Jackson's left said. She was perhaps twenty, with straight brown hair topped by a beaded headband which went straight across her forehead. "My husband and I are off to visit my parents in the countryside. We arrived last night." She became animated. "But if we ever did want to stay downtown, this is where we'd be! Why, the nightlife, the scenery, the shopping ... this lies at the center of it all."

Several heads nodded around the table, and the waitstaff smiled at each other.

Mrs. Jackson said, "I had no idea."

"Well, my dear, if you're going to stay in Chicago any length of time, you should definitely stay here," the dowager Duchess proclaimed. "This is the place to be!"

***

And yet, Mrs. Jackson mused, they'd likely just been witness to a murder.

5

The garrulous old dowager annoyed her. Not only that, she was dangerous. They couldn't dodge too many questions about themselves before rousing suspicion.

So Mrs. Jackson fired a return salvo. "My Lady, what sights should we see first?"

This set the dowager into a stream of recommendations, each with its own set of observations, quips, and amusing stories. It was left for Mrs. Jackson to simply nod, smile, and exclaim from time to time.

As the woman spoke, Mrs. Jackson glanced around the table. Most were dressed in casual finery, ready for venturing forth into the street. The dowager's husband Albert had on a red felt vest which looked handmade, decorated with small wooden beads.

Her interest caught his eye and he glanced down, then grinned, pulling at the bottom of his vest. "You like it? Got this on our travels."

"Oh," the dowager said, "let me tell you about that trip." And so she set off again, to Mrs. Jackson's great amusement.

The Duchess herself wore a simple necklace of golden-brown beads, which as it turned out, were seeds hand-drilled by her husband. "Oh, he just loves making things," she gushed.

Her husband beamed.

"Would take a steady hand, that," Mr. Jackson said.

This sent the dowager's husband into an explanation of the tools he used, with exclamations and witty stories from the dowager along every step of the way.

Once they'd finished eating, Mr. Jackson rose, shaking hands all round. "We're so pleased to meet you! Have a wonderful day." Then to her relief, he took her arm and moved off towards the lobby before anyone could insert themselves into their day.

She giggled at that thought. "You're a master at handling people."

"You didn't do so poorly yourself." The dining room door attendants opened the beveled glass doors for them. "Do you still fancy a stroll?"

"No." Her arm had begun to ache, and the exertion of fending off the dowager fell upon her. She felt suddenly gray, transparent. "Let's go back upstairs." She looked up at him. "I hope you weren't looking forward to it. Going out, I mean."

Mr. Jackson put his arm around her waist, then took her left hand in his, steering her towards the elevators. Which she felt grateful for, as the effort of making the decision seemed beyond her right then. "Not at all, my dear. I'm here for whatever you need."

She hated feeling so weak, hated needing someone to bring her places like some invalid.

"Is she well?" The concerned face of a bellboy swam before her.

"Is a wheeled chair available?"

"Wait here, sir, I'll get one right away."

Her vision cleared. They stood before the array of elevators.

"Here," the bellboy said, and something pressed upon the back of her legs. She sat, placing her hands on the armrests.

"Thanks," Mr. Jackson said, and a rustle of cash followed.

"Thank you, sir!" The bellboy sounded quite pleased.

A group had gathered, yet moved aside when the elevator door opened.

"Let's get you to your bed," Mr. Jackson said. "We've had enough excitement for today."

***

Mr. Jackson felt helpless when his wife sagged in his grasp out by the elevators, utterly grateful for the bellhop's assistance with the chair. He should never have taken her down to breakfast so soon after surgery.

He'd seen sickness and injury many a time, yet it'd always been someone else who handled the details. He'd had to ask his wife how much medication she took, and somehow, he felt he should know.

But he could help his wife into bed, keep watch over her. He could hold her hand, listen to her soft breathing.

It reminded him too much of another bedside, another hand. That scene had ended in death, right in front of him, and he felt a brief instant of terror that she might die as well.

His wife woke well after tea. "Welcome back," he said.

She stretched lazily. "Have you sat there this entire time?"

He shrugged. "The view is lovely whichever way you turn."

"Since when have you become a flatterer?"

"Never. I prefer to speak the truth, when I can."

She smiled at that. "And what will you do now?"

"Read the afternoon paper. Order dinner in our rooms. Converse with my wife. Go to bed early." He stretched. "I am on vacation, after all."

"Do you really travel all over, visiting your properties, as you said?"

"When the need arises."

She smiled, falling quiet for some time. To his surprise, she said, "Do you remember when you captured me?"

He chuckled at that, rubbing the ugly old scar on his upper left arm. "One hardly forgets getting shot."

Her voice seemed playful, but a sharpness lay beneath her words. "You brought that on yourself. If you hadn't tricked me, none of that would have happened."

He felt humbled at the memory. "I suppose I did. Why do you ask?"

She sat quietly for a while. "Who took care of you?"

"Why, my sister, of course. And two of my retainers."

"Those must have been trusted retainers. Everyone thought you were dead!"

He nodded. "They were." He still wasn't sure what she wanted. "Why do you ask?"

"Oh, I don't know — I want to know you better, that's all. I feel like my entire life has been spent trying to kill you." She let out an ironic chuckle. "Yet today I've wakened alive, with you guarding me."

His eyes stung. But he smiled, picking up her hand and kissing it. "I'll be here always, dear girl. For as long as you need me."

***

To Mrs. Jackson's surprise, a knock came at the parlor door.

36

Mr. Jackson went to answer it. A few minutes later, he returned, closing the door behind him. "Duchess Cordelia is here to see you. Should I send her away?"

Mrs. Jackson considered the matter. She felt well, and was still in her day dress. "How does my hair look?"

Mr. Jackson smoothed her hair down on both sides, tucked the back part behind her head, then drew back to survey her. "Perfect."

"Then I feel fit to receive visitors."

Mr. Jackson left, returning a bit later with the dowager Duchess, who rushed to sit beside her. "Oh, my dear, I've been so very worried for you! I heard you'd fell ill after breakfast, and they called for a wheeled chair!" She pressed her hands to the sides of her face, eyes wide. Then she dropped her hands to her lap. "I do hope you're improved?"

Mrs. Jackson felt amused. "I am, thank you."

Mr. Jackson retreated, closing the door behind him.

An awkward silence fell, so Mrs. Jackson said, "I hope you and your husband are well?"

"Oh, Albert's fine — he's off on a walk." The old dowager surveyed her. "I do hope I'm not intruding."

"Not at all. What can I do for you?"

Duchess Cordelia drew back, nose reddening. "My dear girl. I'm here to visit you!" She reached over and took Mrs. Jackson's hand in hers. "My poor dear. You're not used to such things."

37

Mrs. Jackson shrugged.

"Well, where I come from, friends have a duty to help each other, or at least offer support. And although we've just met, I wish to act as a friend."

"That's very kind of you," Mrs. Jackson said, and meant it. "I'm flattered."

The old woman's eyebrows rose, and her mouth dropped open.

Mrs. Jackson said, "A Duchess here, at my bedside, wishing to befriend me?"

The dowager chuckled. "Oh, that. I've never been much for putting on airs. My Duke is dead, the estates sold." She shrugged. "Hardly seems worth all the fuss."

Mrs. Jackson smiled at her. The woman seemed sincere, but she had to be cautious about revealing too much. "I'm honored to have your company."

The old woman's cheeks reddened. "Can I do something for you? Get you anything?"

"Might you ask Mr. Jackson to come in?"

"Of course, my dear." She went to the door to the parlor, returning with him.

"Sir," Mrs. Jackson said, "would you call my lady's maid? The number's on the stand beside the telephone. I was thinking we might take dinner here in our rooms."

From the expression on his face, she knew he was amused at her formality. "My dear, I am ever at your service." He picked up the slip of paper beside the phone, disappearing into the parlor.

From the expression on the dowager's face, Mrs. Jackson knew she'd made a mistake: she'd aroused the old woman's curiosity. "Have the two of you known each other long?"

This question actually surprised her, threw her suddenly back to the night they met. "Why, yes, many years now. Why do you ask?"

Duchess Cordelia appeared flustered. "Uh, well, I don't mean to intrude. Just making small talk."

Perfect! Small talk it would be, then. "How did you come to marry a Duke? That seems so grand."

The Duchess chuckled. "Well, I suppose it was. My family was a very good one, but nowhere near as grand as all that. It was all arranged: both myself and my Duke were the last heirs to survive to that day, and our fathers felt it the best way to preserve our fortunes."

The last to survive? "Oh, I'm so very sorry."

She shrugged. "I was, strangely enough, an only child. My Duke's family suffered quite a bit of tragedy, though." This seemed to dishearten her. But then she brightened. "It turned out well, when you consider everything. It was a good match, and we made the most of it."

Mrs. Jackson smiled at the old woman. "I'm glad for you." But then she felt at a loss as to how to proceed. She didn't want the dowager to begin asking questions again. "Do you have any advice?"

The Duchess beamed, her eyes growing moist. "Oh, if I only had such a sweet nature at your age, to ask for advice!" She grasped Mrs. Jackson's hand in both of hers. "Right now, all you need to do is to rest and get well." She grinned. "Let your young man care for you. Once you're stronger, we can talk all you want." The clock struck seven. "I must dress for dinner. Please take care of yourself."

"I will."

After she left, Mr. Jackson came in. "What did she want?"

"It seems simply to be my friend."

He let out a breath, slumping into the chair Duchess Cordelia had used. "That's a relief."

Her stomach rumbled. "Let's order dinner now, shall we?"

"Ah, yes, my poor dear, you slept through tea. You must be starving!"

She giggled at that, then sat forward, tucking her feet under her knees tailor-fashion. "But I feel stronger somehow. You want to explore that park tomorrow?"

He grinned. "Only if you feel well enough." His tone turned playful. "I will be sincerely vexed at another fainting spell on my watch!"

***

After dinner, Mr. Jackson opened the afternoon news, which had the desk clerk's death on page 8:

CLERK FOUND DEAD AT POSH HOTEL

Police Ruling: "Suspicious"

A desk clerk was found dead at his post yesterday morning at the Myriad Hotel on Lake Shore Drive.

At this time, police have not released the name of the victim nor the cause of death, yet a spokesman for the police department stated the death is considered suspicious.

The hotel manager released this statement: "Our deepest sympathies go to the family and friends of the deceased. The Myriad Hotel offers its full cooperation into the investigation."

The Myriad Hotel, established in 1897, is one of the premier hotels in Chicago, visited by notable and prominent people from around the world. The Hotel anticipates no alterations in service due to this unfortunate event.

Mr. Jackson showed his wife the article. "They ruled it suspicious."

"It certainly seemed that way to me. I hope they find whoever did it soon."

He closed the paper, leaned back, stretched his legs out. Hopefully, the police would have no further interest in them. Once his wife was well, they could speak to the staff as the manager requested.

The manager barging into their rooms the day before like he had still annoyed Mr. Jackson to no end. It was unnecessary. The matter certainly wasn't urgent, and the police seemed well-equipped to pursue the culprit.

His wife looked pale, and while the dark circles around her eyes had improved, he didn't like seeing them there. "How's your arm?"

"I might need some medicine soon."

He rose to fetch the bottle. "Same amount?"

She considered the matter. "Yes, I think so. It makes me much too sleepy, but it's time for bed in any case." She grinned up at him. "A good night's sleep should help."

***

The next morning was a fine one: a blue sky, children playing in the sun, trees fluttering in a light breeze. Cars chugged past, steam spouting from tail pipes. A bird flew by.

The couple sat arm in arm on a park bench. Mrs. Jackson took a deep breath, savoring the clean, crisp air. So different from home, with its perpetual gloom.

She felt much more rested today, clearer-minded. And she was reminded of the manager's request.

At first, it seemed odd that the owner would ask two strangers for help in a police matter. Yet on further consideration, she'd decided that if the owner's priority was to keep things quiet, the fewer people who knew about the matter, the better.

"Last night, you said the police ruled the matter suspicious," Mrs. Jackson said. "But you never offered your opinion."

"I suppose it could have been natural," Mr. Jackson said. "But the man was so young. And his face so pale. I agree with the ruling: this feels like foul play."

The man's face was certainly an unnatural shade. If only she'd had a chance to examine the body more closely.

Mr. Jackson said, "The teacup on the floor was quite evocative. Poison, perhaps?"

She squeezed his arm, a sudden wave of fondness passing over her. "If nothing, you are sharp of mind. I hesitated to take tea with breakfast for that very reason."

"As did I. But poisoning suggests the offender knew the person, or at the very least, his habits. Unless, of course, he wished to kill us all."

Mrs. Jackson smiled at him as they rose, moved along the sunny path. "Yet everyone made it from the table alive. Point well-taken, sir."

For her, the conversation was merely chitchat, a way to pass the time. The man was dead: surely the police would care for the situation.

It felt good to stroll in this park for a moment, to smell the breeze, watch the clouds pass. Forget everything which had led up to this day. Never in a thousand years could she have anticipated being in this city, strolling in this park today, arm in arm with this man — much less being married to him. How things had changed!

Mr. Jackson tipped his fedora at a passing couple, then said, "Yet who would wish to kill a desk clerk?"

She smiled to herself. "I'm sure the police ponder the very same question." She let go of his arm, pulled out her cigarettes, the matches with them. "Light one for me?"

His eyes narrowed. "Very well." He handed a cigarette to her, lit it. "But I won't have this in our rooms."

"Fair enough."

They continued to walk side by side as she smoked. "What do you think is happening back there right now?"

"At the hotel? I have no idea."

"No, back home."

He chuckled. "I imagine quite a lot." He stopped then, faced her. "My dear, you must forget it all. Consider yourself reborn. None of that," he made a wild, sweeping gesture, "will bring anything other than grief and trouble." He began to walk, and she followed. "For us, today is all that matters."

She dropped the cigarette, stepped upon it, then held onto his arm. Could it be possible to make a clean break with the past? In some things, perhaps. But not others. "Is there a pharmacy nearby?"

"I can ask if it's important. Is there something you need today?"

Mrs. Jackson considered this. "A day or so probably won't hurt."

"If you're sure."

"I'm sure." He truly seemed concerned for her welfare. "If you'd like to find the address, we can visit the pharmacy the next time we venture out."

***

Mr. Jackson strolled back towards the hotel with his wife. To his relief, her cheeks had good color, and the dark circles were almost gone from around her eyes. Rest had been all she needed.

The streets were busy, and so was the hotel lobby. Tourists gazed at the murals above the rosewood paneling, families stood around planning their day.

Leading his wife by the hand, Mr. Jackson made his way through the throng towards the front desk to fetch their room key. An older woman scrubbed the wooden floor in the hall beyond: a dark stain lay there.

The new desk clerk was an eager young man with blond hair, just bloomed into adulthood. As he handed over the key, he said, "Anything else you need, sir?"

Suddenly, a list of things they needed appeared in Mr. Jackson's mind. He chose the one with highest priority. "Where is the nearest pharmacy?"

The clerk wrote on a pad, then handed over a slip of paper. "There's the address." He pointed past Mr. Jackson's left shoulder. "Three blocks that way, just past the gun shop. It's open until nine tonight."

"Excellent," Mr. Jackson said, slipping the paper into his jacket pocket. On to number two. "I wonder if we might speak with the manager."

The young man seemed uneasy. "I hope all is well?"

"It is. Very well indeed. We just need to speak with him on a private matter."

Relief crossed the man's face. "Very good, sir. You'll find him in his office," he pointed behind him, "down the hall. The door is on your left."

The couple edged past the scrubbing maid and moved down the hall.

"Mr. Flannery Davis, Manager" lay marked upon the door. Before they reached the open doorway, the manager's voice came forth in a shout: "By thunder!"

Mr. Jackson peered inside. "Is all well, sir?"

The manager glanced up, an open lunch-pail marked with his name in front of him. "Someone's been at my lunch again! I'd always blamed that poor foolish clerk, but —"

Mr. Jackson stared at the man, horrified. "Where do the staff take luncheon?"

"Continue down the hall and turn right. The lunchroom is downstairs. Why do you —?"

"Don't touch a thing!"

Mr. Jackson raced down the hall, but as he got to the corner, screams emerged from below. He turned to his wife, who remained standing in the doorway, mouth open. "I'm afraid we're too late."

6

Sergeant Nestor stood observing the lunchroom turned crime scene. He'd deliberately placed himself near the couple, who'd inexplicably been witness to two murders in three days.

A clump of uniformed officers stood around the contorted body of a blonde girl. Agnes Odds, age eighteen, worked at the Hotel these past three years. Rented a room in the basement. No one knew of any family.

The rest of his men were busy. They gathered evidence, took samples, photographed the body, spoke with witnesses.

Across the lunchroom, the manager paced up and down, wringing his hands. "I shall be ruined! If this gets out, no one will stay here. We'll all lose our jobs!"

The staff gaped at him.

The manager stopped, turned to them. "Not one word of this to anyone, not one. You hear?"

Fearful nods all round, then the room filled with discussion.

Sergeant Nestor thought the man was likely right. The rich men who owned places like this tossed their employees away like day-old trash at a moment's notice. But the manager's order would now make it much more difficult to get any of these people to talk.

One of the officers stood near a distraught middle-aged woman with black hair. "She just came in, started eating, and got the most horrible look on her face! Oh, I'll never forget it!" The woman began sobbing, her friends around her.

Mrs. Jackson seemed notably unaffected by the sight. "I suspect strychnine."

Her husband nodded, uneasy.

The sergeant said, "The manager told us you knew this might happen."

"We went there to see him," Mr. Jackson said. "The manager mentioned his lunch had been tampered with in the past. He'd suspected the clerk who died yesterday of being the culprit. It occurred to me that if this clerk had been pilfering lunches, then perhaps he wasn't the true target."

The sergeant nodded. "And this young woman was?"

Mrs. Jackson shrugged. "Perhaps. Although the manager claimed his lunch had been tampered with today as well."

This didn't seem like something a killer would want known. The sergeant turned to an officer beside him. "Bring every lunch to the lab, including the manager's. Search them all for poison. And put a round-the-clock guard on the food pails until the killer's found."

"That does seem wise," Mr. Jackson said.

The couple weren't acting like killers. And they'd been upstairs with the manager at the time of death.

Mrs. Jackson said, "Is there anything we might do to help?"

She sounded too eager. And he didn't believe for one minute she was a professional investigator. "I don't want you involved." He pointed at them. "I don't want you two to do any nosing about whatsoever. Stay out of it. You understand?"

Mr. Jackson chuckled. "Very well."

Sergeant Nestor regretted his harshness. He didn't want to discourage people from coming forward. "But if you **do** hear something —"

"We'll inform you at once," Mrs. Jackson said, with a smile which made the sergeant more than a bit envious of her husband. She took her husband's arm. "Let's see to the manager before he has a coronary."

As the couple strolled away, Sergeant Nestor watched her go. How did **that** fellow get a woman like **her**?

He walked over to the group of police standing around the dead woman. One of his officers glanced past him towards the couple. "You suspect those two?"

"I suspect everyone." A couple of people claiming to be private investigators — one a woman! — appearing right as a rash of deaths began. And then offering help — on their honeymoon?

They found the body. And now they wanted to be part of the investigation. "Something tells me they're going to be trouble."

***

Mr. Jackson and his wife walked over to the manager, who was most distressed indeed. "Let me assure you, sir, that we have NEVER had such goings-on here before. I want to —"

Mr. Jackson raised his hand. "We're quite confident in your hotel. I've stayed here many a time. But there is a matter in which you might aid us."

The manager's shoulders slumped. "How much do you want to keep quiet?"

Mr. Jackson felt amused. "Nothing so crass. We're both gentlemen here!"

Relief crossed the manager's face. "How then may I help?"

"Might you recommend a discreet private surgeon? For my wife. We were told to contact one in a few days."

The manager glanced at Mrs. Jackson's sling. "We have one on retainer. No charge to you whatsoever."

"Very good," Mr. Jackson said. "You may call him in whenever it's convenient." He gestured to the group still milling about. "I'll let you get back to your staff."

"Thank you, sir," the manager said. "And please, not a word to the other guests?"

"Of course not," Mrs. Jackson said. "I dislike even to think on it." She glanced at the contorted body and shuddered. "How horrid!"

"I'm most grateful. If you need anything — anything at all, you have only to ask."

***

Mrs. Jackson considered the pretty little blonde who'd sold her the pack of cigarettes a day earlier lying crumpled on the floor.

Whatever the girl might have done, killing her this way was wrong.

Once the manager left, Mr. Jackson said quietly, "My ... wife. I feel astonished. I never thought such words would ever come from my mouth."

Mrs. Jackson chuckled, taking his arm, and the couple moved towards the lobby. "And yet here we are."

They strolled through the lobby, past the grand fountain, towards the elevators. Then Mr. Jackson spoke. "It surprised me that you mentioned strychnine."

"Oh?"

"And offering to help a second time. I'm not sure either was wise. I'm certain the sergeant suspects us."

She felt amused. "He's the sort to suspect everyone." She smiled up at Mr. Jackson, and to her surprise, he blushed.

"Well," Mrs. Jackson said. "Our stay has become much more interesting than I would have ever thought."

7

The couple ate lunch in her room. Then Mrs. Jackson took her pain medication and lay in bed reading the paper. "Tell me about Chicago," she said, "since you've been here before."

Mr. Jackson downed his coffee, then shrugged. "It's a place, much like any other. The police here are competent; the criminals, somewhat less so. Only alcohol is forbidden. But of course, because alcohol's forbidden, everyone wants it. There are speakeasies on every corner, if you know where to find them. But many of the police will look the other way, especially if you hand them a fiver."

Mrs. Jackson nodded.

"And there's every amusement one might possibly imagine." At that, his face brightened. "Oh, my dear, we must see the talkies."

"Whatever are talkies?"

"Pictures which talk and move! And they often have the most wonderful music. Like a play, only the characters are projected upon the screen using light. They're all the rage!"

Mrs. Jackson folded the paper, astonished at the idea. She felt positively sheltered! What else in the world went on that she knew nothing about? "That does sound interesting."

"Then we shall go, just as soon as you feel well enough."

Her wound did hurt quite a bit, especially when she moved her arm. And she hadn't quite gotten the dose right on the medication: it still made her sleepy. "Perhaps in a few days."

"Anything you desire is yours, my dear; you have only to ask."

She recalled his blush. Which, although attractive and sweet, conflicted with what he'd said just before they arrived. "May I ask something personal?"

"You may ask anything at all."

"Why are you being so kind to me? The truth."

He leaned his elbows on the table, rested his chin on his closed hands. "Because, strange as it sounds even to me, I like you. I find you fascinating. I'd like to spend more time with you." He leaned back, crossed his arms. "And I always try to speak the truth, as much as I can." He relaxed, just a bit. "I'll understand if you need to be alone, after everything that's happened, but if you do need me, even to talk with, I won't feel it a burden."

She felt abashed. "I don't mean to be ungrateful. And I'm sorry for not trusting you. It's just —"

Mr. Jackson put his elbows back on the table, his face in his hands. Then he raised his head and smiled at her. "Things certainly could have gone better."

In spite of how awful she felt right then, she chuckled, wiping her nose on her handkerchief. "It certainly could have." She took a deep breath and let it out, feeling better. "So what do you think of these murders?"

"Ever the investigator, are we? Well, it's possible that someone had it in for the young lady, badly enough to try again when failing the first time. The real question is why? Once we know why, well, then who is never far behind."

This threw Mrs. Jackson into some thought. Why would someone poison a girl's lunch? And with strychnine, of all things. "If they simply wanted to kill her, they could have killed her down in the basement. Or used some more peaceful solution. Or some longer acting agent which would kill many hours later to hide their involvement."

But they didn't. "Is it possible this killer meant to send a message to another member of the staff?"

Mr. Jackson smiled. "There you have it."

"But why kill a young woman? She had her whole life ahead of her." She shook her head, eyes stinging. "This is wrong."

***

Mr. Jackson surveyed his wife. Her eyes were drooping. She'd be asleep soon. But the young woman's death had affected her. He knew his wife well enough: if he didn't persuade her to remain still, she'd begin searching for the girl's killer despite her injury.

"I can't just lie here — a girl is dead! And to kill her in this way?" She shook her head, face turned away. "There must be something I can do."

"What you can do is rest. You've just had surgery."

She slid down in the bed, eyes sleepy. "But to do nothing seems wrong."

He shrugged. "The sergeant strictly forbade our involvement. He already suspects us as it is."

"Yet the manager asked us to speak with the staff. They need us."

What should he do? "How about this: once you're asleep, I'll walk through the hotel, take a look around. It's likely someone will speak with me."

She beamed. "If you should find a clue to these murders, I suppose the time I have to spend asleep won't have been entirely wasted."

He laughed. "If you think my amateur questioning adequate."

"Don't be silly." She gave him a sleepy smile. "I can't wait to see what you discover."

"Shh, dear girl. Rest now." He moved his chair beside her bed, rested his hand upon her forehead. "Sleep. You must get strong. Then we can find this killer."

She smiled, eyes closed.

He sat, stroking her thick black curls for a long while as he watched the clouds play over the sky.

As soon as his wife seemed firmly asleep, Mr. Jackson slipped out, locking the door behind him with the "Do Not Disturb" sign on.

He stood in the hall, hesitant. Normally, he wouldn't leave someone so recently injured unattended.

But in her eyes, this girl's murder had changed everything. She'd never truly rest until the matter was resolved.

So he set off.

The halls were quiet, as was the elevator. But the lobby bustled with people. Bellhops brought gleaming brass carts filled with luggage to and fro. Valets brought keys, escorted men to their cars. Families strolled the walkways on the upper levels, guarded by wrought iron, gazing and pointing at the sights.

Beside the busy front desk, the dining room doors stood open, its tables full of people reading, drinking coffee, and talking. Waiters and maids moved to and fro.

A handsome young man with dark hair played the grand piano in the center of the room.

While Mr. Jackson had stayed at this hotel before, he'd been a guest for the night, simply using it as a place to sleep while conducting business. Downstairs, he'd only visited the dining room and lobby. If they were to stay at the Myriad Hotel until his wife recovered, he wanted to see what it had to offer them. And perhaps he'd learn something.

He moved back across the wide marble-tiled lobby, past the glorious fountain and the grand curving stair. As he passed the foot of the staircase, a large grandfather clock upon the first landing struck two.

Just past the stair was a wide expanse. Down a hallway to his left, people waited for the elevators. On the wall straight ahead was a soda bar. Ahead and to his right (near the front of the hotel) lay the gift shop. Between the two, a hallway marked "Library" stood before him.

The soda bar's counter stretched eight feet in and twenty long, made of polished rosewood trimmed in brass. Brass barstools with cushions of black leather stood at intervals. Golden light came from decorative bulb fixtures in the ceiling.

Six small tables nestled in the room. The one in the far back right held a couple sipping drinks through paper straws.

The soda jerk — a boy of perhaps sixteen — glanced up from wiping the bar. "Care for a glass, sir?"

"What do you have?"

The boy gaped at Mr. Jackson, eyes wide. "We have over two hundred flavors — more if you combine them!" He gestured at the bottles lined floor to ceiling along the wall, each labeled with their syrup's flavor.

"That's quite impressive." He peered at the array. "How about lemon and ginger?"

"Right away, sir."

Mr. Jackson sat on a bar stool, watching the boy work. "I don't recall this place being here the last time I stayed."

"How long ago was this?"

"Several years now."

"Well, sir, they put this in before I come to work here."

A large stuffed owl stood perched at the corner ceiling in an alcove above the many bottles. A rosewood door with a brass knob had been set diagonally into the corner directly underneath, which seemed an unusual arrangement for any building.

"That's a fine specimen," Mr. Jackson said, pointing at the owl.

The boy smiled to himself, his cheeks coloring.

"Your work?"

The boy twitched, focusing on the counter. "No, sir. Been here as long as I remember." He handed over a glass of soda. "Two bits."

"Would you put it on my tab? Hector Jackson, 3205."

"Of course, sir."

The soda was quite good — not too sweet.

A light fell upon the owl, and its eyes began blinking. Mr. Jackson laughed, pointing at it. "Would you look at that!"

The boy glanced over his shoulder. "It does that sometimes." His tone became falsely bright. "Would you like anything else, sir?"

This was interesting. Out of curiosity, Mr. Jackson asked, "What else do you serve?"

The boy hesitated. "Ice cream sodas, with real imported vanilla. Best in town."

Mr. Jackson leaned back, surveying the lad. "My wife might like that!" He extended a hand, which the boy shook. "A pleasure to meet you," he peered at the boy's name-tag, "Thomas. I'm sure I'll be seeing you again. Oh, and when you submit that, give yourself a nickel tip."

The boy's face brightened. "Yes, sir! Thank you, sir."

Very interesting indeed.

Mr. Jackson walked a pace or two into the lobby then to his right, just out of the boy's view. He surveyed the room, watching people go up and down the wide stair to the second floor. The lobby was just as full as it had been a few moments before. Yet at that moment, not one of any of the people in the huge room were workers.

He'd wondered more than once about the lack of staff when they'd arrived. Now he thought he'd stumbled upon the answer.

8

As he continued on past the crowd waiting for the elevators, Mr. Jackson considered the mystery of the owl. Its blinking clearly was a sign, but to whom?

He whirled, returning to the place he'd stood. The valet stand outside was clearly visible. An older, olive-skinned man now stood there, dressed in a valet's uniform. The man returned his gaze with a set face and a slight nod.

A chill ran down his back.

Clearly something untoward went on here in the hotel. Would it be something worth killing for?

Mr. Jackson moved back towards the elevators. Whatever was going on, they certainly wouldn't tell him of it.

Past the elevators, he came upon the striped pole of a barbershop. The barber swept the floor, glancing up as Mr. Jackson arrived. "Can I help you, sir?"

Mr. Jackson had his personal manservant Mr. Vienna, who normally took care of such things. Yet he felt he might learn more were he to visit here. "Just taking a look-round, but now I know you're here, I'll return."

The man smiled. "Very good, sir."

The man hadn't been downstairs with the others. "Are you employed here, or do you rent the booth?"

"Oh, I rent. Not interested in being employed by others, sir. Keeps my options open."

Mr. Jackson smiled. "Good man. That's the spirit."

"Let me know if you'd care for a freshening up before dinner," the barber said. "I get several in starting a bit after tea."

"You know," Mr. Jackson said, "I may just take you up on that." His manservant had been hired for breakfast and dinner, but he wouldn't be round until seven. And if many men would be here, this might be a perfect opportunity to learn more.

"Very good, sir. I look forward to seeing you."

A ladies' hairdresser appeared next, a glassed-in affair with a fine beveled-glass door. Past that, a wide hall went to his right, marked with a sign:

Dog Grooming & Veterinary Services

A smartly dressed woman with golden blonde hair said, "Excuse me."

He moved aside while she and three dogs with hair matching hers pranced past and down the side hall to another beveled-glass door.

"Astonishing," Mr. Jackson murmured.

Through windows to his left, a courtyard appeared, with an extensive, luxurious garden. He glimpsed moving water past foliage. A conservatory? Perhaps his wife might like to visit there.

When he reached the end of the hall, a small tree at the back corner caught his eye: glossy green leaves of a sort he'd never seen before. Instead of one vein down its center, these leaves had three, equally spaced.

"Extraordinary," Mr. Jackson said to himself.

The main hall went to the left, and so did he, the view of the courtyard soon lost. To his right, he passed three offices, then a wide hall transected his. The sign on the left pointed to the kitchens; to the right, the hall ended at an open door.

A brown-haired man dressed in brown khaki work clothes stood past the door on a metal balcony. He turned as Mr. Jackson approached, taking a lit cigarette from his mouth as he leaned on the black metal railing. His name-tag said: Eugene. "Need help, sir?"

"Just taking a stroll. I was curious as to what was out here."

Eugene smiled to himself, taking another drag from his cigarette.

Stairs led down both sides to a ramp wide enough to hold several trucks. A few parked there, while a rather large truck backed in, guided by a man wearing blue denim overalls. On the side, it said:

Carlo Brothers Imported Olive Oil

The Best of Italy

"What do you do here?"

Eugene shrugged. "Me? Maintenance."

"I thought they had maids for that."

Eugene snorted in derision. "I don't scrub floors. I fix what needs fixing."

"Ah, forgive me. I see. Like the trucks?"

"More like the drains." He sucked at his cigarette, blew out smoke. "But whatever. Yesterday I fixed a hand rail. Sometimes I go round to check for rats."

"Do you get many here?"

"Rats?" He let out a short laugh. "Not if I can help it. Wouldn't be in business too long if it got out we had rats, now would we?"

Mr. Jackson chuckled at that. "What all do you use for them? Traps?"

"Naw," Eugene said. "Manager doesn't like that. He's got me setting out poison." He shook his head with a slight frown. "Just makes my job harder."

"In what way?"

"That stuff's dangerous. A dog or cat gets hold of it — it's not pretty." He shrugged. "Means I have to put the bait back where the bigger animals can't find it."

"Does seem like more trouble than it's worth."

The truck had disappeared, and the sounds of men unloading came from below.

"I know you," Eugene said. "You're the bloke that found the body. You were in the lunch room, too."

"I was indeed," Mr. Jackson said. "I'm very sorry for your loss."

Eugene shrugged. "Everyone thought the new guy was stealing people's lunches. But Agnes? A sweet little tomato, that. Don't know why anyone'd bother hurting her."

"Not too bright, then, I take it?"

He chuckled. "A few cards shy of a deck, if you get my meaning. She'd do whatever you asked, but you had to tell her exactly what." A hard look crossed his face for an instant. "That fellow that got killed — not even here a week, and he had her pinned in a corner." He shook his head grimly. "I set him straight, all right."

"How chivalrous of you."

Eugene gave Mr. Jackson a startled glance. "I didn't kill the man. Just pulled him off her. Poor little gal had the shakes after." He let out a breath. "If he hadn't got killed first, I'd have put it on him."

Interesting. Mr. Jackson leaned a hand on the railing. "Did they know each other? Before that?"

"Not that I know of."

"How was she after that? Before she died, of course."

Eugene shrugged. "She seemed fine. Always smiling. Always with a good word for others." He lapsed into a morose silence, staring out over the loading area.

"It's strange," Mr. Jackson said after a bit. "The manager said someone was at his lunch today."

Eugene's eyebrows raised. "Well, now that makes me glad they put a guard on them. If you can't eat in peace, what else is there?"

Mr. Jackson turned at a clanking noise. The doors to a large elevator — which he hadn't noticed — opened. A maid rolled a covered cart out and towards the kitchen.

"I'll leave you to your smoke," Mr. Jackson said. "A pleasure meeting you."

Eugene nodded. "Likewise."

Mr. Jackson went to the main hallway and stood listening to the noises of the kitchen.

Was it just a coincidence that the major component of rat poison here was strychnine?

He shook his head, unsure what to make of it, before continuing to the right. More offices appeared, and in the corner, another wide hallway went to the right, this time marked "Laundry."

He turned left to follow the main hall once more, which was marked:

Ladies' Spa

Indoor Pool

Gentlemen's Sauna and Baths

Lobby

All was as marked, and he came back round to the lobby once more.

"May I help you, sir?" The blond young man still stood behind the front desk.

Perhaps this was his chance to learn something. "How are you faring?"

"Sir?"

"Everything that's happened must be terrifying."

The man hesitated.

"I know, you aren't supposed to speak of it. But my wife and I found your coworker. The man who was here. We know everything that's happened — well, I suppose as much as anyone else does." He held out his hand. "Hector Jackson."

The clerk shook his hand. "Lee Francis."

Mr. Jackson grinned. "Used to be an investigator, once upon a time." At that, he shrugged. "Just offering an ear. Your manager seemed to think it would help." He glanced around; no one stood waiting. "I won't bother you any —"

"Not at all, sir," Lee said. "It would help, sir. To talk. I didn't know the other clerk; he'd just been hired. But I did know Miss Agnes." His face fell. "It's been hard."

Mr. Jackson nodded. "To stand at your post even so ... that's bravery."

Lee straightened. "I don't feel brave, sir. I don't want to be fired. Lots are talking about getting other jobs. But there aren't many these days. And if they hear you're looking, they cut your hours to nothing and hire someone else." This seemed to dishearten him. "My wife's with child. We need the money."

"Why would someone do such a thing?"

The young man rested his hand on the edge of the counter. "That's what I've been trying to understand. I don't know anyone'd want to hurt either of them."

"Has Agnes had trouble with anyone here?"

Lee shook his head. "If she had, I'd not have known it, sir. One of the maids might've; she was friendly with them all." Suddenly his face changed. "Jackson, right? I almost forgot; you have a message." He handed over a folded slip of paper.

Mr. Jackson took it and nodded: the surgeon would be by to see his wife later today. "Thanks. Never you fret: I'm sure the police'll have it sorted soon." Mr. Jackson glanced around; a woman waited with a pile of luggage. "I should let you return to your work. But any time you want to talk, just look me up."

"Yes, sir. Thank you, sir."

Mr. Jackson went to the dining room and took a seat at an empty table. People had been asking questions of him since he'd arrived; perhaps if he sat here long enough, someone would answer a few of his own.

9

Instead of making assumptions or forming suspicions, Hector Jackson preferred to approach things — as much as a grown man might — with the open mind of a child. What had he observed? What did he observe now?

George, the young waiter from breakfast the other day, came to his table. "How may I help, sir?"

"Coffee, heavy cream, no sugar," Mr. Jackson said. "And the paper, if you please." George had been in the sun recently. Too much sun, if the skin behind his neck spoke true.

The staff in the dining room moved like people free from care and worry. Their voices were cheery and warm.

Yet the occasional flinch, the sideways glance when passing, all spoke volumes: *is this the one who may murder me next?*

Not the most comfortable of working environments.

And not the most congenial place to stay, either. They had a week's credit here at the hotel. But should he move his wife somewhere else? Or would it put too much strain upon her?

"Your coffee and paper, sir." The waiter's left sleeve rose, revealing a recent rope burn.

"A boating man, I see," Mr. Jackson said.

George appeared astonished. "However did you know?"

Mr. Jackson smiled up at him. It seemed obvious. But he liked this fellow, so he said, "You've been in the sun recently. The sun at your back, I'd say. Many prefer to sail so, and it looks as if the wind kicked up." He pointed to the man's arm. "I've had many such in my day."

George stood speechless.

"What size is your boat?" And how a waiter afforded one was a question Mr. Jackson wished to ask, yet refrained, feeling it perhaps too intrusive.

At that, George relaxed. "It's my pa's, sir. We went out for the week end. Well, rightly, it's my grandpa's, but he rarely sails anymore."

A matron across the room had a hand raised, trying to get George's attention. Mr. Jackson gestured towards the woman with his chin. "I'll let you attend to your work. But I'd love to talk boats, any time."

George beamed. "Right, sir. Any time!" He gave a small bow and hurried off.

Mr. Jackson didn't feel any more enlightened than he had, but he'd made a friend. Perhaps one who might know more of the place than he. With a close family and an elderly yet well-to-do grandfather.

Who worked as a waiter?

The news had nothing as yet about the most recent death, which didn't surprise him — the afternoon paper wouldn't be out for another few hours. But he was surprised to see nothing more about the first one. A man dying at a place like this drew reporters like flies to honey.

Which made him consider: who would be harmed by such unwanted attention?

The manager and staff first came to mind. Then he recalled the owner, the "man you wouldn't want to make angry."

Were these deaths part of a feud among the staff, with these two caught in the middle? Or could these deaths be a strike against the hotel? A way to "encourage" the customers and staff to abandon it, perhaps instigated by some rival chain?

Chicago was a city known for its rivalries. Low-class gangsters and uncouth men of all sorts struggled for power here, only partially kept in check by the cops. Was the Myriad Hotel's esteemed owner one of them? Or had he gotten himself on the wrong side of their battles?

He sipped his coffee, which was excellent.

"Might we join you?"

Mr. Jackson looked up from the news. The old couple from breakfast the day before stood there. He rose to greet them. "Please. I insist."

The three sat.

The dowager Duchess glanced at the paper. "What news?"

Mr. Jackson folded the paper and passed it to her.

"Cordelia," her husband Albert said, "where are your manners?" Then to Mr. Jackson, he said, "Forgive her, sir. She's been too long among the common folk."

Mr. Jackson smiled to reassure them. "Not at all, sir: I had finished with it. I hope you both are well?"

"Quite well," she said, her lined cheeks coloring, "and yourself?"

"Splendid."

"And your wife?"

Now that was amusing. "She's resting at present. But much improved."

"Ah, yes," the old man said, "her injury. Very good."

It was obvious they wished to ask all the juicy details. So he said, "You mentioned the last time we met that you stay here at the hotel."

"Oh, yes," the dowager Duchess said. "Three years now. Wouldn't have it any other way."

"So you must know the staff quite well."

"Most," Albert said. "The young man who died —" at this, he seemed genuinely sorrowful, "no, he'd just been hired. Most distressing."

"And all the hotel's various amusements as well."

"Ah," he said, as if he'd finally understood something.

George came up then, speaking to Albert. "Would you like to order anything, sir?"

Albert glanced at his wife. "Tea for us both, with lemon. Steep it well." Then he turned to Mr. Jackson. "Yes, this place is a marvel! Did you know that there's a glassed-over courtyard with a simply wonderful garden? They let you help tend it."

That must have been what he saw earlier. "Is that so?"

"Yes! I so love trimming the flower bushes. That's the one thing I missed from the estate, tending the garden."

Mr. Jackson said, "What made you decide to move here? If it's not too intimate a question."

"Oh, no, not at all," Albert said. "I —"

"Well, Bertie —" the dowager said, clearly uncomfortable.

"Now, Cordelia, never you fret," her husband said. "I was only going to tell Mr. Jackson that the estate was yours," he turned to Mr. Jackson, "you see, we married late in life, after the death of her husband. Old money, that. But times are changing. No children to inherit, and the house just got too big for us." He pattcd his wife's hand. "We're much happier here."

It could have been the lighting, or perhaps Mr. Jackson's imagination, but the dowager Duchess didn't look quite so pleased to be here as her husband seemed. "Do you also like tending the garden?"

She gave a one-shoulder shrug. "I'm content to watch him work, although I am very fond of flowers."

Albert beamed at her. "I make sure she's well-supplied."

Mr. Jackson couldn't say why, but he felt something more was at work here. "What other amusements catch your fancy, my Lady?"

Her face brightened. "I do so love reading. The library here is a delight! And if there is some item not in stock, why, the Main Library is just a short trip away."

"What sorts of books do you favor?"

"Oh, she loves any sort of book imaginable," Albert said. "She was ever so bright as a child. Much more so than I."

"My word," Mr. Jackson said. "So you've known each other quite some time."

"Indeed we have." The old man glanced at his wife fondly, his cheeks coloring. "Indeed we have."

"Perhaps one day you might show my wife and I around," Mr. Jackson said.

"I would love to."

Cordelia leaned forward. "How is your wife, really?"

Mr. Jackson shrugged, not sure how much to reveal. "Rest is what she needs right now. Her medicine makes her sleep, which is for the best."

"Poor dear," Cordelia said. "Well, you be sure to give her my regards."

***

No one else approached, and to his dismay, the dowager and her husband never left. After his coffee, Mr. Jackson returned to his suite, leaving the old couple chattering about a book on flowers.

His wife stood on the balcony, a lovely picture in shadow framed by the sunny lake beyond. The breeze fluttered her gown and hair.

He put his hands beside hers on the wrought-iron railing. "How do you feel?"

She shrugged. "I'm not sure how to feel, to be honest." She smiled to herself. "What did you discover?

He hesitated, taking a deep breath. "They're hiding something. An underground speakeasy, I'll wager."

"Oh?"

No restaurant, no matter how grand, needed that much olive oil. "And I wonder: were these killings meant to discredit the hotel? If so, then the real question is why?"

Mrs. Jackson considered this. "Are the deaths related?"

He shrugged. "Our young clerk was no paragon of virtue. A dockworker told me the man tried to force himself upon the young lady who next perished."

"Really."

"Yes. The whole matter angered him greatly."

"Do you suspect him?"

"I suspect everyone. And the staff is afraid. There's talk of leaving."

She nodded soberly. "So if we are to help our host, it would be best done quickly."

He let out a laugh. "You are relentless! I'm glad to have you on my side this time." He surveyed her archly. "Quite formidable."

At that, she gave him an amused smile, holding up her injured arm. "Imagine once I'm well!"

The surgeon arrived at half past four. He was a man in his middle fifties with a solid, competent air to him.

Mr. Jackson stood watching as the man examined Mrs. Jackson's arm, asking her to move it, testing its sensation. "The wound looks to be without infection," the doctor said. "How is the pain?"

"Improved," she said. "I cut the dose the surgeon gave me to half, as it makes me much too sleepy otherwise."

"That's a good sign," the doctor said. "I'll return next week to remove the stitches. In the meantime, you may move the arm, as long as there's no pain when you do so." He smiled at her, as one might to a young girl. "Yet be gentle with yourself. It'll take a while to fully heal, and you'll need rest for your body to do so."

Later, the doctor took Mr. Jackson aside. "I've never seen such a botch job in my life."

Mr. Jackson felt alarmed. "Is she in danger?"

"Danger?" The doctor shook his head. "It seems to be healing well enough. But this is going to leave a terrible scar. How did it happen?"

Mr. Jackson hesitated, unsure how much to relate. "A ... tragedy occurred just prior to our marriage. Family members were murdered. She was injured, and ... I wasn't consulted on the matter until after the surgery."

The doctor stood there, mouth open. "I had no idea, sir. My deepest condolences."

Mr. Jackson nodded, pensive.

"The manager said you were on your honeymoon. I hope —"

Mr. Jackson stared at the man, horrified. She'd just had surgery. How could anyone be so cruel? Yet he understood where the question came from: other men might have taken advantage. He smiled to himself. "I've been kind to her."

The doctor patted Mr. Jackson's arm. "Good man. I've been married thirty years now. Kindness is a sure investment."

"Her arm. What can be done?"

The doctor retrieved a notepad and fountain pen from the breast pocket of his tweed jacket. "I'll give you the name of a specialist. A bit of a journey, but he's the best at this sort of thing. A real artist. He'll have her fixed up in no time."

"We're most grateful."

The man handed the paper over. "You should wait until the wound's fully healed to contact him. Scars often improve over time."

Mr. Jackson reached into his pocket for a tip.

But the man waved him off. "Not necessary, sir, it's all paid for." He took on a jolly demeanor. "One of the perks of fine hotel living."

It was then Mr. Jackson remembered. "You're on retainer."

"Indeed I am," the doctor said. "So if you need anything at all, don't hesitate to call."

When Mr. Jackson told his wife what the doctor had said about her wound, she snorted. "Figures."

He laughed at her tone. "Well, at least we have a few weeks before we need to make a decision."

"Perhaps in that time, we can find our poisoner."

Mr. Jackson chuckled, shaking his head. "You're like a bloodhound in your persistence." He smiled at her fondly. "If much more attractive."

Her cheeks colored as she glanced away. But a shy smile touched her lips, quickly fading. "You don't understand: I need to be useful, especially now."

He sat beside her, rested his hand on hers. "Usefulness is overrated. What you need is to recover." A wave of grief and fear for her washed over him. "I won't lose you too."

She hesitated, then her shoulders slumped. "Oh, very well. You and the doctor have persuaded me, for now." She stretched upon the bed with a smile. "The beds are so beautifully soft. That's some compensation for my enforced idleness." Her smile turned into a wicked grin. "Will I be served in bed from your hand? Perhaps strawberries and whipped cream would do."

This made him laugh out loud. "My dear, you may have any pleasure your heart desires." He rose. "In fact, I'll call for it now."

She sat up. "I was only teasing."

"Very well." He sat beside her and put his arm round her shoulders. "Do you want to take tea here, or downstairs?"

"Downstairs, I think. I've had enough of being in here for now."

10

By the time the couple descended for tea, the dining room was packed — every table full, every seat in the lobby taken.

The cook, a forty-year-old brown-haired woman, glanced at Mrs. Jackson's arm and smiled at the couple as she passed by. "Afternoon tea, or early supper?"

"We're here for tea," Mrs. Jackson said.

"Very good," the cook said. "I'll have a girl get you set up, sir, ma'am."

"Much obliged," Mr. Jackson said.

Mrs. Jackson watched as a young maid arranged teacups, saucers, a pot of tea, and a large plate of small sandwiches from the buffet area onto a tray. Then she and Mr. Jackson followed the woman to an empty table in the soda shop.

A young man behind the bar waved to Mr. Jackson when they entered.

He seemed to make friends everywhere he went. However did he do it?

Mrs. Jackson was intrigued by the owl, especially after Mr. Jackson told her — in whispers, once the maid left — about the blinking. And the tremendous array of bottled flavors!

She'd never had a "soda" before, so they resolved to return for one after dinner. "This is the most marvelous hotel," she said. "By all accounts, one might never have to leave!"

"That seems to be the aim," Mr. Jackson said with a grin. "More profits for them!"

"Indeed," Mrs. Jackson said. "And I must say, well done!"

They feasted upon the sandwiches — egg, but like nothing Mrs. Jackson had seen before. These were made with whole quail's eggs, hard-boiled and sliced thin upon a spicy creamed spread. She wiped her mouth. "Delicious!" She took a sip of her tea. "I never imagined such a dish."

Mr. Jackson nodded. "The chefs in Chicago are superb." He drained his teacup and poured another. "There are dozens of restaurants in the downtown area alone." He took a sip, then became animated. "We must visit them all!"

She enjoyed his enthusiasm, yet ... "Do you think it wise to stay here that long?" She leaned forward to speak more softly. "Perhaps once we find this killer, we should be on our way."

Mr. Jackson's face sobered, and he put down his cup, leaning over to cover her hand with his. "I would never do anything to put you into harm." He leaned back, gazing off to one side. "No one in all the wide world is looking for Hector and Pamela Jackson. And even if they were, the chance of finding us here is astronomical. So relax, my dear. Enjoy yourself!" He gave her a fond smile. "Life's much too short to do otherwise." He sipped his tea. "I propose we stay until you're completely well, then we'll decide."

She felt relieved that they might not have to rush away. That they might truly be safe here.

Just then, the old man from breakfast the other day walked by, and spying them, hurried inside. "My dear Mr. Jackson! I was just going to check on the garden." He turned to Mrs. Jackson. "Your husband expressed an interest in touring the gardens." The man glanced back and forth between them. "Would you care to join me?"

The couple exchanged a glance, and she nodded. Gardens seemed a pleasant enough diversion.

"Why, of course," Mr. Jackson said. "Just as soon as we're done here."

"By all means, take your time."

***

Just then, the manager strode in, coming to their table. "There you are!"

Mr. Jackson felt amused. Not wanting to force his wife to rise, he remained in his chair, just as he had when Albert arrived. "Indeed we are, sir. How may I help you?"

"Well, I told the owner about the situation here, and he's come to tour the facility today and talk with the staff. Stay the night. It'll settle their worries, I think. He'll probably take dinner in his room, but he wants to meet with you both sometime after."

Mr. Jackson felt surprised. "I'd be honored." He glanced at his wife. "If my wife is well enough, of course."

"Certainly. Mr. Carlo knows the situation — you being on your honeymoon and all — but he did so want to at least meet you."

"It's settled then," Mr. Jackson said.

Albert had watched the exchange without a word, arms crossed.

The manager glanced at him, then back at Mr. Jackson. "I'll let you get back to your tea, then."

Mr. Jackson said, "Would you like to join us?"

"No," Albert said, "My wife needs me to have something sent up from the gift shop. I'll meet you back here afterward."

Mrs. Jackson beamed at Albert. "We're looking forward to your tour."

At that, Albert smiled, but it seemed forced. "Be right back."

Mr. Jackson pondered the exchange. "I don't think Albert Stayman likes the manager very much."

His wife nodded, eyes far away, seemingly lost in thought. But then she said, "I imagine living in such proximity, anyone would have a spat from time to time."

He chuckled at that.

She put her cup down. "I'm ready to go, as soon as your friend returns."

As they waited for Albert, the cook came by their table. "How did you enjoy your tea?"

"Lovely," Mrs. Jackson said. "I particularly liked the sandwiches."

The woman blushed. "I'm so happy you liked them!"

Mr. Jackson said, "How kind of you to stop by!"

"I try to meet everyone while they're here," she said. "It helps me to know how to improve."

This seemed quite admirable. Mr. Jackson held out his hand. "Hector and Pamela Jackson."

She took his hand and curtsied. "Miss Goldie Jean Dab, sir."

Mrs. Jackson said, "Have you worked here long?"

"Ten years in May, and a nicer place to work you'd never find."

Albert walked up, and the couple rose.

"Just leave everything here," Miss Dab said. "I'll get a girl to take these for you. I hope you have a wonderful stay."

Mr. Jackson and his wife followed Albert across the lobby. To his surprise, a wide hallway with a sign marked "Gardens" lay behind the stair. Down the hall, a beveled glass door appeared.

The door opened into a vast courtyard. Trees both large and small dotted the area, with flower bushes around them. A path of grayish-brown brick wound past these. The air was warm, humid, and fragrant.

During the chill of winter, Mr. Jackson thought he and his wife might enjoy this as much as walking the park.

Some trees held fruit! Mr. Jackson turned to Albert in astonishment.

"This is really a conservatory," the old man said. "It gets so cold here in the winter, thus the glass roofing."

Mr. Jackson nodded. The buildings stretched high above them, white clouds in the deep blue sky. The roof itself reminded him of some giant crystal, inlaid with pipes of brass. "Do you get much snow?"

"Yes, but it melts straightaway. Heated, you see."

As they continued on, a pond appeared to the left. Lily pads, brightly colored fish, and smooth oval rocks lay in the clear water. Further on, a short waterfall dropped from a small brook as the path wound slightly upwards to another garden area.

"This is lovely," Mrs. Jackson said.

The old man beamed.

They went on for some time. Off in one corner, the small tree he'd seen before appeared upon a raised area in the corner by the window, far from the path with no other plants in its bed. Mr. Jackson said, "What is that tree? I glimpsed it from the hallway."

The old man smiled broadly. "Ah, the snake-wood tree! Fascinating. I picked up seeds while traveling, the summer before we came here. The tree which used to be in that spot died, so I took it out for them and planted this here."

Mr. Jackson thought it a remarkable plant. "I've never seen leaves like that before."

"It's a most singular tree," the old man said, yet he seemed uneasy. "It'll produce these pale greenish flower bursts, and fruit of a sort once it's old enough — in about fifteen or twenty years." He let out a laugh. "I might even still be around to see them." At that, he sobered. "Nothing you'd want to eat, mind you. I imagine it tastes terrible. But quite pretty." He gestured towards the path. "Want to see more?"

Mr. and Mrs. Jackson moved along as directed. "You seem to enjoy plants quite a bit," Mrs. Jackson said.

"I do! Much more reliable than people." He laughed softly to himself.

Mr. Jackson said, "You mentioned you've known your wife since childhood. Did you live there at the estate?"

"Oh, yes. I was the groundsman's son. It was my father gave me the love of growing things. I did up all the flower beds, planted most of the trees there ..." His face turned wistful. "It was a beautiful time."

"And she was an only child," Mrs. Jackson said. "I recall her saying so."

Albert said, "Yes, she was."

Mr. Jackson smiled. "And so the groundsman's son became the groundsman. And the little girl, a woman."

The old man smiled to himself. "Indeed."

Mr. Jackson said, "Were you in love with her even then?"

Albert gave Mr. Jackson a startled glance. "Yes, I suppose I was. Of course, then, she was too far above me to even consider it. She married, they split the time between their properties. I saw her less, to be sure, but it seemed we had a bond even then. It was all very proper, though. I never dared speak until her husband's death."

Mrs. Jackson said, "What happened?"

"It was his heart."

"I meant, how did you end up marrying? Her being so far above you and all."

The old man glanced away, his cheeks coloring. "I suppose it just happened. She needed a great deal of help after her husband's death. I provided all the flowers for the funeral. A grand thing, it was, befitting the Duke. But it cost more than the estate could bear."

Mr. Jackson said, "And now you've been married these past three years."

"Close to four, now. Three of them here. We traveled the world at first." He paused for a moment, then said, "I don't much care where I live. So long as I can be close to her, that's good enough for me."

Mr. Jackson found that touching. "Thank you for taking us round." His wife's face looked relaxed and happy for the first time in a long while. So when he next spoke, it was with sincerity. "We love this garden."

"So you might stay, then?"

Mr. Jackson said, "We haven't decided as yet. But we'll most certainly enjoy it while we're here."

"I'm so glad." Albert seemed relieved. "I've always felt a certain pride in my gardens, a responsibility to the things I grow. Like a parent who brings children to the world — to tend and care for them."

Mr. Jackson nodded, fascinated by the man's assertions. "I never considered it that way. But then, I've never been a gardener."

"Well, any time you want to come with me, you're more than welcome. I usually come out early, before breakfast. Not so many people then."

"I'll keep that in mind." They approached the door, and his wife took his arm as they returned to the lobby. "Thanks again for the tour," Mr. Jackson said.

"Don't mention it." Albert pointed to their left. "Have you seen the library?"

"Not yet," said Mr. Jackson.

At the same time, Mrs. Jackson gasped. "You have a library?"

"Did your husband not tell you? Come this way. Cordelia is there now." He moved ahead, and they followed.

Mrs. Jackson whispered, "You never said anything about a library!"

Mr. Jackson replied, "I never knew you enjoyed them!"

"I do," she said. "Very much so."

They reached the long hall to the library. "Then it seems you could just as well recover here as anywhere else."

His wife beamed. "Perhaps I shall like staying here after all!"

The library was rather large, stretching (it seemed) clear the length of the building's front on that side. Narrow windows of beveled glass let in the dim light of an early evening. The room was decorated in the same dark rosewood and brass which graced the rest of the building. The lampshades were finely-made panels of cobalt glass, and the chairs were upholstered in black velvet.

The dowager sat upon a chair, a pile of books on the round table before her. She rose once she saw them. "How lovely to see you!"

Several people looked up.

"Oh, silly me," she said, half as loudly, "come, let me show you around." She and her husband moved ahead.

"This is her garden," Mrs. Jackson whispered.

Mr. Jackson thought the idea quite amusing.

Bookshelves eight feet high ran around the walls of the entire room, and many more lined up within.

Mrs. Jackson's eyes were wide with wonder. "I love it!"

"I'm so glad you like it, my dear," the dowager said. "I'm here almost every day. I would most enjoy your company." She turned to the rows. "Here, walk with me and look around."

So they did, moving well to the back to browse the collection there.

The dowager whispered, "I never asked. What brings you to the city?"

Wishing he had a dollar for every time he'd been asked this, Mr. Jackson whispered, "We're on our honeymoon!"

"My congratulations to you both," the dowager said, and her husband nodded.

Mrs. Jackson smiled at her. "Thank you!"

The old woman smiled to herself. "I do so love a good romance tale." She focused on Mr. Jackson. "When did you know she was the one?"

He felt himself blush; why, he wasn't sure. "Well. It's perhaps awkward."

"Oh, come now," the old woman said with a quiet laugh. "I can't imagine you doing anything remotely improper."

He grinned. "You'd be surprised." He hesitated, casting a glance at his wife. "It's a rather long, somewhat embarrassing story. Yet I had chance to see her legs, and —"

Mrs. Jackson went crimson, and Albert glanced away.

"Oh, this **is** a good tale," the dowager whispered.

"- and I have to say I was smitten." For an instant, he felt foolish. But he collected himself, meeting his wife's eyes. "For quite some time I could think of little else."

Mrs. Jackson stood gaping at him.

"Well," the dowager said with quiet glee, "this is fascinating! One day you must tell me the entire story."

A woman's voice came from above: "Dinner will be served at eight. Hotel guests have a standing reservation. Others should come to the concierge desk at once to make reservations if they wish to dine."

A grandfather clock stood at the back end of the room: five minutes to seven. "We should dress for dinner," Mr. Jackson said to no one in particular. "It was good to see you," he said to the old couple. "And thank you for the tours."

They went out into the lobby. Mrs. Jackson said, "So — all this time?"

Heat rushed to his face. "Yes."

She didn't reply.

As they waited for the elevator, he said, "I wonder — when you return to the library — if you would mind learning what you can about the snake-wood tree."

"Oh?"

"It very much interests me."

She bristled. "Well, the library stands ready. Tomorrow you're welcome to go look for it."

"I'm sorry. I didn't mean to imply —"

The elevator opened, and people went in and out, but they stood off to one side, facing each other.

"I'm no servant," Mrs. Jackson said. "I never have been, and I never will be. I didn't ask you here; I allowed

95

you to come with me. I even married you, at your advice, even though now it seems you've lied about the reasons. But if we are to be married, then let us see each other as equal. And speak true to each other in all things, as you claimed you prefer. Or we can part ways."

He felt abashed. "Forgive me. I meant no harm." Then he felt dismayed. He'd taken a vow, long ago, to protect this woman. One he could never break. Had he driven her away? "I — I've never done this before."

She surveyed him for a long moment, then rose on tiptoe to kiss his cheek. "All is forgiven." She took his arm. "I suppose we shouldn't leave Mrs. Knight and Mr. Vienna waiting for us."

As his wife had suspected, the maid and valet stood waiting in the hall to dress them for dinner. Mr. Jackson introduced them to each other. "Would the two of you be so kind as to purchase nightclothes for us? We seem to have forgotten to pack ours."

Mrs. Knight and Mr. Vienna exchanged a quick, amused glance. "They'll be in your rooms after dinner, sir," Mr. Vienna said.

The couple went down to dinner shortly thereafter. This time, they were seated with newcomers, and ate in silence as talk swirled around them.

Mr. Jackson felt a certain agitation. Why did he share that story? He should have known it would upset her.

But there was no help for it. He considered what might be best to say. Finally, he ventured, "I hope you're well."

Mrs. Jackson smiled then. "I am, so far as that goes. I was simply pondering a matter best left out of dinner conversation."

"Ah." She must mean the murders, all accomplished by food. At least so far. "Indeed."

"Yet I did wonder when the next event might occur."

"Oh?"

She put down her fork, and turning towards him, spoke for his ears alone. "Unless you believe the young woman to be the true target."

It was a good question. From all accounts, the young lady hardly had the capacity to poison someone on her own. And it seemed doubtful she'd have knowingly poisoned herself. At least, not in a room full of her friends.

So the poisoner was still in the hotel with them.

Would someone poison their own coworkers? Yet who had access to the lunch room, other than employees?

"How are you enjoying your meal?" George, the young boating man turned waiter, stood across the table holding a tray full of dishes.

Mr. Jackson glanced at his plate: much of the food remained. "Forgive me; I'd become distracted. It's very good."

"I'd be happy to get you something else if you prefer."

"Not at all." Mr. Jackson looked round the table. Some of the guests were sampling desserts, others had left. His wife's empty plate held the remains of a lemon-cake. "Would you care to try a soda?"

She nodded, and he turned to the waiter. "Would you get us —"

George's body jerked violently, and he dropped his tray with a crash.

11

Mr. Jackson, shocked speechless, stared at the empty space George had just occupied.

Mrs. Jackson leapt to her feet. "Doctor!"

Her shout jarred him from his immobility. Heart pounding, Mr. Jackson followed his wife to George, whose face twisted in agony.

"I'm a doctor," an elderly man said.

Mrs. Jackson, who now knelt beside the young man, looked up at the old doctor. "It's strychnine."

"Good gracious," the doctor said.

"There's a veterinary around the corner there," Mr. Jackson said. "Might they have something which could help?"

The doctor stared blankly back. "They might." He hobbled out.

Meanwhile, George's back arched, his eyes frightened, pleading. Mr. Jackson stood helpless, hands shaking, not knowing what to do.

"Peace, good sir," Mrs. Jackson said, brushing hair from George's forehead. "We'll stay with you." Then she called out, "We need an ambulance!"

The room scattered as people ran about. The doctor returned, out of breath. "I have activated charcoal and tannic acid," he panted, "and a mouth syringe."

"Do what you must, sir," Mr. Jackson said, feeling relieved.

The doctor fumbled with the containers, his hands shaking, as everyone watched. But finally he got a solution down George's throat in between the young man's spasms.

Mr. Jackson said, "How long will this take to work?"

"It depends on how much he ingested and how long ago." He bent over the man, trying to get his attention. "Did you eat or drink anything?"

George's face was red with the strain. "Lemon-cake," he groaned.

A woman began screaming, "AAAAA! AAAAAAA! I had lemon-cake!" People began running towards her in agitation.

Then another screamed, "I did too!"

Mrs. Jackson stood. "SHUT UP!"

The first woman seemed shocked, then offended. "Well, I never!"

"If you'd been poisoned, you'd be dead by now," Mrs. Jackson snapped. "So take your hysteria elsewhere."

Mr. Jackson had never respected anyone more than he did his wife right then.

She returned to kneel by the man's side. George seemed to be less agitated, then a spasm twisted his face once more.

Mr. Jackson looked to the doctor, who shrugged. "Never treated this before. Only read about it. But I'll try a bit more of the charcoal. A glass of water, sir, if you please."

Mr. Jackson fetched his own, and the doctor gave the young man a slurry of the activated charcoal by mouth. After George swallowed it, the ambulance arrived, along with the police.

As the ambulance men carried the young man off, the sergeant said, "You two again."

"They saved me, sir," George moaned. He looked at Mrs. Jackson. "Thank you."

The dining room was in an uproar. Everyone had questions, concerns, expressions of outrage. Mr. and Mrs. Jackson retired to their original seats at the table to await the inevitable visit from the sergeant's men.

"Quick thinking, that," Mr. Jackson said to his wife, hoping his voice wasn't shaking as much as it sounded. "Well done." He took a deep breath, trying to calm himself. "I'd hate to see such a fine young man succumb to this poisoner."

She nodded, face pensive. "This person — whoever it is — becomes more bold."

"Surely this is being done by a man," Mr. Jackson said, "is it not?"

The sergeant, who'd been standing across the table where the young man once lay, looked over. "Poisoners are generally women. Or shall I say, women who kill are usually poisoners." He shook his head wearily. "Every woman in this building is now a suspect."

***

Once the young man was carried off, Mrs. Jackson felt weak, shaky, and her arm ached. The sergeant questioned them, then said they could go, warning them not to leave the building.

So the couple went across the lobby to have their ice cream sodas.

"This is quite good," she said. "And I love how it fizzes so. It's a unique flavor!"

Mr. Jackson didn't reply.

She peered at him. He still seemed shaken by the night's events. "Are you well, sir?"

"I don't rightly know," he said, staring at the table. "I feel as if something of great moment has happened —"

A laugh burst from her. "A man almost dying would certainly qualify!"

He glanced up at her, and the look in his face made her feel chagrined. "Forgive me." Then what was happening dawned on her. She leaned forward, eyes stinging. He'd given up a great deal for her, perhaps more than he should. "Truly. I should not have laughed. It was wrong for me to do so. I'm sorry."

At that, he sighed, shoulders slumping.

"Listen to me," she said. "Everyone reacts to sudden events in different ways. You must not berate yourself, or feel shamed at how you did so." She reached across with her good hand to take his. "The doctors here are excellent. All will be well."

A bit of a smile touched his lips. "I'm supposed to be comforting you."

She shrugged. "We're married, are we not? I believe it goes both ways."

Once they'd finished their sodas, they returned to their rooms. "Another eventful day," Mrs. Jackson said, sagging into a chair.

"The reporters couldn't fail to feature this," Mr. Jackson said, an edge to his tone. "I feel certain whoever is doing this targets the management."

"But why? Why not kill whoever the person has it in for?"

"Maybe he — or she — has it in for all these people. Perhaps the deaths are related. But what does a new, unprincipled desk clerk, a young woman who by all accounts wouldn't hurt a fly, and a waiter from a good family have in common?"

"The hotel," Mrs. Jackson said. "They all work the day shift. Might this waiter have been sampling lunches as well?"

"You don't kill someone for stealing your lunch," Mr. Jackson said, sounding annoyed. "Not unless you're mentally deranged. Besides, the dinner pails are under guard as well."

"The lemon-cake." Mrs. Jackson kicked her shoes off, put her feet up on the side of her bed. "Individual cakes. Easy to poison one without harming others. And I imagine easier to hide a strong taste in a lemon-cake than in some other food."

"Indeed."

"So your young waiter swipes a lemon-cake —"

"Wait," Mr. Jackson said. "George served me earlier today. After luncheon."

"So he was on an extra shift, perhaps," said Mrs. Jackson.

"Yes."

She leaned forward. "So maybe the poisoner doesn't know this. Maybe this order was to go to someone in particular, but the young man —"

"Swipes the lemon-cake," Mr. Jackson said, then chuckled. "Apt way of putting it."

Mrs. Jackson smiled at him. "And almost pays dearly for it." Her heart sank. "How will we know who the cake was to go to? That's our next target, I'd wager."

Mr. Jackson rose. "Stay here. I'll relay this to the sergeant. Surely they have someone searching the kitchens by now."

She held out her hand, feeling suddenly afraid. "Be careful."

"Oh, dear." He gave her a soft smile, taking her hand in his. "First, apologies, now this? Who are you, and what have you done with my wife? I'd almost think you were concerned for me."

She ignored his levity: he had to understand. "If this poisoner thinks you pursue him — or her, they might become desperate. Take care."

He leaned over to kiss her forehead, something he'd never done before. "I will."

She really needed her pain medication by this time, but she didn't dare sleep until he returned. So she took a part dose, struggled into her new nightgown, and — more than a little frightened — sat up in bed to wait for his return.

***

Locking the doors to their suite, Mr. Jackson hurried down to the lobby.

105

A huge crowd milled about. Reporters and high-class men demanded answers which the young officers guarding the doors to the dining hall couldn't give. Off by the chairs, a few richly-dressed ladies were being fanned and fawned over by their retainers.

Mr. Jackson felt a deep gratitude that he traveled with a sensible woman. She'd saved George with her quick action.

Pushing through the crowd, he approached the dining hall doors. A familiar-looking officer glanced at him and said, "Ah, yes — the sergeant asked me to let you through."

Exclamations of outrage followed him inside — some quite rude — and he felt glad when the door shut behind him.

The dining hall swarmed with police. The far area was filled with people being questioned. Off to one side, Albert Stayman paced as the dowager Duchess sat speaking with an officer. The area where George had fallen was being measured and photographed, much as the area around the front desk had been.

The sergeant walked over to meet him. "I hope you and your wife are well."

"She's resting," Mr. Jackson said. "The pain medication makes her sleep." He smiled to himself fondly, imagining her face peaceful.

"Very good," the sergeant said. He seemed to relax a bit. "First marriage?"

"My first," Mr. Jackson admitted. "My wife was widowed."

"I'm sorry to hear that. I did wonder at such a lovely young woman marrying so late in life."

Mr. Jackson felt amused. "Thank you." He realized then what was happening. "This isn't a social call."

Sergeant Nestor snorted.

"Very well," Mr. Jackson said, feeling weary. "What do you want to know?"

"You were speaking to the young man when he collapsed."

"He stood across the table." He struggled to recall the scene. "I don't remember what we spoke about. But then he fell."

The sergeant nodded. "And your wife came to his aid."

"Yes, and I'm grateful for it. I happened to speak with him this afternoon. Most congenial young man."

"Oh?"

"We both like boating."

"Certainly fortunate that she did. And that a doctor was present who knew the remedy. And that the veterinary was still open."

"It was indeed," Mr. Jackson said. But something in the sergeant's tone disturbed him. "You aren't suggesting she had something to do with this?"

"You've been seen about quite a lot for a man on his honeymoon."

Mr. Jackson felt confused. "I don't understand."

Sergeant Nestor frowned, his tone sarcastic. "I knew your kind the moment I lay eyes upon you. You speak with a young, handsome waiter — thrice — then he falls, your wife the one to 'save' him. That's one way to win back your attentions."

Mr. Jackson felt dismayed. "You have the situation mistaken." A chair stood nearby, and he leaned upon it. "My wife is just days from having had surgery. The hotel surgeon instructed her to complete rest, but —" he took a breath to stop his voice from shaking, "my wife is, if nothing else, headstrong. Enforced idleness chafes at her." He felt then as if rambling, and collected himself. "Our relationship is none of your concern. But if you think she would harm someone out of petty jealousy, then you know nothing about her!"

Normally, he was a calm man, but at this, Mr. Jackson felt angry. "And do you really think I would betray a woman I **married**? I made vows, sir, ones I would not break even on pain of death. I came to offer help, but I will not stand by as my wife and I are slandered."

The sergeant gave him a soft smile. "I had to ask these things." He hesitated a second, then held out a hand. "I would be glad for your help."

Mr. Jackson hesitated, still feeling annoyed. But then he shook the man's hand. "Very well. What do you want?"

"What most here want. To find our murderer."

Mr. Jackson felt unsettled. "May we sit?"

"Of course."

He sat, heart pounding. Had he been so transparent? Worse yet, should he have stayed beside his wife, not left her up there alone? He'd thought collecting information would help her feel as if something were being done.

The sergeant let out a breath, "Don't berate yourself. You're in a difficult situation — I'm sure you've done your best." His tone turned businesslike. "I need you to focus on the matter at hand. I know you've spoken with the staff. What did you learn?"

"Learn?" He had actual proof of very little. "The staff are — naturally — disturbed by these events. There's talk of leaving for new employment." He didn't want to mention his suspicions of an underground speakeasy just yet, so he shrugged. "That's all."

Then he remembered. "I did hear something of interest. A dockworker — Eugene, I believe his name was — told me that the desk clerk who first died had tried a few days earlier to force himself upon the young lady who died next. This dockworker is also the rat-man. I don't know if it matters, but —"

The sergeant's face didn't change. "We'll speak with him."

"Do you know yet how the clerk died? After seeing what the waiter endured, it doesn't seem like strychnine to me."

"The coroner is still investigating," the sergeant said. "It may take days to learn the truth."

"Well, then," Mr. Jackson said. "How may I help? Do you wish us to investigate?"

"Absolutely not," the sergeant said. "Stay out of it. I'll let you know if I have any further questions."

"But my wife and I believe —"

Voices raised above the crowd from behind, and Mr. Jackson turned towards them. The beveled glass doors were open; two men walked in.

Sergeant Nestor went to meet them. Fine clothing both, yet one had stiff, dark hair, deep-set dark eyes, and an imperious manner. The other, who resembled the young waiter, although much older, looked worried, and after getting some information from the sergeant, hurried away.

That must be the father, Mr. Jackson thought.

The remaining man seemed to be lecturing the sergeant, who appeared to be giving as good as he got.

When the doors opened yet again, the manager rushed over to the two with a cringing, subservient mien.

Mr. Jackson rose, walked over, and held out his hand. "You must be the owner of this establishment. Hector Jackson at your service, sir. A pleasure to finally —"

The man's jaw dropped. "However did you —"

"- meet you," Mr. Jackson continued, speaking over him.

The owner seemed flustered, yet shook hands. "And you, sir." He glanced around. "I take it you discovered the first body?"

"I did."

"Davis here has kept me informed."

Mr. Jackson felt relieved at him not mentioning the arrangement he had with the manager, at least not in front of the sergeant.

The owner turned to the sergeant. "This has gone on long enough. No more arguments. You know what to do."

12

The next morning, the front page of the paper read:

MURDER AT THE MYRIAD

Cook arrested for poison

Mrs. Jackson put down the paper, dismayed. "Surely the cook isn't to blame for this! That's much too simple an answer."

Mr. Jackson nodded. "The owner insisted they arrest someone."

"This is bad," she said. "Two murders — and one attempted — in four days? And by the look of it, missing the real target each time. I fear another death will come soon."

He nodded. "After our servants are through with us, shall we spend the day in the city? I don't fancy staying around the hotel today."

There came a knock at the door. Mr. Jackson rose. "They're here early, it seems!"

But it was the dowager Duchess come to call. Mrs. Jackson wasn't sure whether to be amused or annoyed that without so much as asking, the dowager pushed past Mr. Jackson and into the room.

Mrs. Jackson did, however, feel very glad that Mrs. Knight had found her a proper nightgown!

"I'm sorry to disturb you so early," the dowager said, glancing at them both. "But my Albert is in a state of agitation! I've called the doctor, who's with him now. In all my years, I've never seen him like this!"

"Come in, sit down." Mr. Jackson sat on the bed. "Whatever has distressed him so?"

The dowager Duchess said, "That's just it, he won't say. I think it was the unpleasantness last night. It's entirely unnerved him!" She looked to Mr. Jackson. "He learned last night of the young lady's death — Agnes, I believe it was. She used to run errands for us. He was very fond of her and of the young man who fell ill last night. Poor dear, he hasn't slept a wink. I thought for certain you might be able to help — he's quite taken with you."

"Why, certainly," Mr. Jackson said. "What room are you in?"

"Thirty-two twelve," she said, rising, "just down the hall and around."

Mr. Jackson stood, tightening the belt on his striped robe (courtesy of the hotel). "Well, then," he said, "let's see what this is about."

**

Mr. Jackson followed Duchess Cordelia down the hall and around the corner to Albert's rooms.

On the walls hung artifacts and souvenirs from around the world. Books sat on every surface possible. In the parlor, a small hand drill with a wooden handle sat upon a bookcase full of books on plants, along with a dark blue mortar and pestle. A row of three satiny gray buttons a bit larger than a nickel hung down a strip of red cloth the size of a bookmark pinned to the wall behind them.

On going into the bedroom, they found the old man weeping on the bed. But when he glanced up, he began to berate his wife. "How dare you bring him here!"

"But Bertie," she said, "you're so upset! I thought he might be able to help."

The doctor who'd seen Mrs. Jackson the day earlier stood by. "Merely overwrought — I've given him a sedative. He should feel better once he wakes."

"Thank you, doctor," the dowager said. She turned to her husband. "Don't be angry, dear — we're just concerned for you."

"I don't want your help. The situation is catastrophic! Intolerable!" He put his face in his hands. "Ohhh," he moaned. "Why has Fate cursed us so?"

"Well, if you do need anything, sir," Mr. Jackson said, "I'll be right around the corner for the next hour. But we planned to go sightseeing. Should we delay?"

Albert's face took on a sudden chagrin. "No, you go. I'm sorry for being such a bother."

"Not at all, sir," Mr. Jackson said. "I hope you feel better." He turned to the dowager. "Poor fellow. Overwrought indeed. I'd stay with him if I were you."

"As I intended. Where did you plan to go today?"

"We might visit the young man in the hospital. But after that, I thought to take my wife to the Main Library. She does so love books."

"Splendid! Well, you just have a marvelous time."

***

The couple went out for breakfast at a little pastry shop nearby, and Mrs. Jackson treated herself to a jelly donut with whipped cream.

"You know," Mr. Jackson said, "when we do visit the specialist surgeon, we must send mail."

"Of course." That would be the perfect opportunity. Anyone investigating where the mail came from would have a jolly time searching in the wrong city. That thought made her smile.

"Where would you like to go afterward? You'll need somewhere quiet to recuperate. I have a lovely little property in Tuscany."

She gasped at the idea of traveling overseas. It was what she'd always dreamed of. "That sounds wonderful!"

Mr. Jackson gave her a fond smile. "I'm so glad you think so."

A man wearing a brown work uniform walked in, going to the counter. The woman behind the counter lit up when she saw him.

Mr. Jackson turned behind to follow her gaze, and smiled at them.

"Someone you know?"

"A man I met at the docks."

The man and woman stood flirting for a few minutes, then the woman handed over a bag. He paid and left without noticing them at all.

The woman came over to their table. Her name-tag read: Helen. "Did you need something?"

Mr. Jackson smiled up at her. "Just saw someone I know, that's all."

Her eyes grew wide. "You know Eugene?"

"Just met the once," he said. "We're staying at the hotel."

"How wonderful! Then I suppose you know the dowager Duchess. She knows everyone."

Mrs. Jackson felt surprised at this. "You know Duchess Cordelia?"

She giggled. "Of course. Me and Eugene play dominoes with her and Mr. Stayman in the evenings sometimes."

Mrs. Jackson said, "I don't believe I've ever played that!"

"Well, next time you'll have to join us," Helen said.

"We wouldn't want to impose," Mrs. Jackson said.

"No! Not at all," Helen said. "Whoever wants to come is welcome. The maids come play with us too from time to time." She smiled at Mrs. Jackson warmly. "We'd love to have you."

Mr. Jackson said, "How are you and Eugene acquainted?"

"We're to be married," she said, showing a cute little engagement ring.

Mrs. Jackson took Helen's hand, admiring the ring. "It's lovely! Congratulations."

The woman beamed. "Thank you."

Mrs. Jackson said, "What does your fiancé do there?"

"Maintenance," she said. "Clearing drains, mostly. They're giving him the dirty work still, but he hopes to move up soon."

"That sounds good," Mr. Jackson said. "Does he like it there?"

Helen shrugged. "All but the manager. Constantly in everyone's business. 'Just let me do my job,' Gene says, about every time he comes home."

Mrs. Jackson felt surprised. "Really."

"Yes!" Helen dropped her voice to a whisper, leaning over to speak privately. "Everyone hates the man. Wouldn't surprise me at all if the next bit of poison went to **him**!"

13

After the couple ate, Mr. Jackson flagged down a taxi to take them to the hospital. There they found the young waiter abed, his parents beside him.

When George saw them, he smiled, reaching his hand out. "Here they are! My benefactors."

His parents stood, turning to the couple. Going past them, Mr. Jackson took the young man's hand and shook it. "I hope you're improved."

Their eyes met, and to Mr. Jackson's surprise, George's cheeks reddened. "Much."

"We're much obliged to you, sir," George's father said. "The hotel doctor told us your quick thinking saved him."

"It was entirely my wife," Mr. Jackson said, looking into George's eyes. "I must admit the suddenness of his malady took me so aback, I hardly knew what to do."

The older man turned to Mrs. Jackson then, taking her hand in both of his. "Then I am forever in your debt.

He's my only son." He stopped for a moment, head turned away.

Mrs. Jackson smiled at him. "You're most welcome."

There were other chairs in the room, on the other side of the bed, so Mr. Jackson said, "May we join you?"

"We insist."

The couple sat then, Mr. Jackson towards the head of the bed. "What happened? It was all so sudden."

"It was," George said. "I broke a lace, so I'd gone in to take a break. There was a long row of room service trays to go up, and the kitchen girls were busy putting lemon-cakes on them. I sat down off to the side to thread a new lace in. I couldn't see the trays from where I sat, but all the girls went past me to get back to their work. I got done threading my lace, and I got up to go. The trays to go out were still there. Right then, Miss Goldie Jean went down the row and said one of the cakes had a bubble — did I want it? She was a-swapping it out and other than the bubble, it looked fine. Well, of course I said yes!" At that, he faltered. "Is it true? Did she poison me? I've never done her a wrong, ever."

"I don't believe so," Mrs. Jackson said.

The older man's face darkened. "Young lady, why don't we let the courts determine such things? She gave him the cake, and now he lies here."

Before she might speak, Mr. Jackson put his hand upon hers. "My wife means no disrespect, sir." He clasped her hand and rose. "We'll let your son rest now."

Once they were outside, Mrs. Jackson said, "I hope I'm wrong."

"I do too," Mr. Jackson said. "But I don't think you are."

Mr. Jackson took his wife to the pharmacy there at the hospital to fill her prescription. The pharmacist puzzled over the paper Mrs. Jackson presented him. "Too much of a dose to fit into a pill."

"Oh, I just take it with water," his wife said.

The pharmacist, an attractive older man with brown hair, grimaced. "This must be so bitter!"

"It is," Mrs. Jackson said. "But it's always been. Is that unusual?"

The man blinked in confusion. "No, I suppose not." He peered at the script. "It's essence of tea! Among other things, of course." He mumbled as he went down the list. "And you're to steep this how long? My word! The tannic acid alone would pucker you for sure." He chuckled. "Well, if this is what you're prescribed —" He glanced up at her. "And you feel well?"

"Entirely, other than this," she said, holding up her arm. "And the surgeon just checked me yesterday."

The pharmacist chuckled. "I presume you're supplied with medication for that."

121

"Oh, yes," she said. "I have plenty."

"Very well. Have a seat, and I'll get this for you."

As they waited, Mr. Jackson felt sure his wife was right. "Not only is the cook innocent, but more deaths are sure to follow."

Mrs. Jackson said, "The poor woman! Slandered, led off in chains to sit in some cell. How will she ever find employment again?"

"We'll help her, my dear," Mr. Jackson said. "If we can prove she didn't do this, they'll have to reinstate her."

"Unless they plan to make her an example." Mrs. Jackson sounded bitter. "It's unjust."

Mr. Jackson put his hand on hers. "It is. But let's put that aside for now and try to enjoy the day."

"I'll try. But we must prove her innocent," his wife said. "I won't be able to rest until we do."

After some time, they were presented with a paper sack full of smaller sacks, along with an instruction page. Then they took a taxi to the Main Library.

His wife seemed enthralled with the sheer number of books in the building, and for a long moment stood staring in joyful astonishment. The look on her face held Mr. Jackson's gaze so that for a while he forgot all else.

Then she met his eye and gave him a real smile, the first since they'd come here. "Let's look around."

They passed row upon row of novels, then factual books on every subject imaginable. They came to the books on plants. There were so many!

His wife stood peering over them. "This is what you wanted, is it not?"

"It was," he said, "but we may look at any you wish. We have no schedule to keep."

A red-haired man stood behind a cluttered counter perhaps ten yards off. A sign hung from the counter's front, labeled "Natural History."

Mrs. Jackson approached the man. Curious, Mr. Jackson followed.

"Thank you," his wife said as he approached. Then she turned to him. "I'll return shortly."

The librarian said, "Your wife?"

Mr. Jackson watched her as she went. "Indeed."

"Lovely lady, I may say."

Mr. Jackson chuckled. "Thanks."

The man poured himself coffee. The cup still had sugar in the bottom, yet he put in more.

"You must like sugar," Mr. Jackson said.

The librarian grinned. "I guess I do."

Then Mr. Jackson recalled what he came here for. "Do you have any books on the snake-wood tree?"

"Let me look." The librarian went to an array of small drawers behind him and pulled one out. Inside were dozens of cards, which he began to page through.

"We do have one, but it's been checked out. But we have more general ones on trees which may be helpful." He took a card out of the drawer. "This way."

Mr. Jackson followed the man down a row of books. The man stopped, peered at the numbers on the spines, squatted to retrieve a thick one on the second shelf from the bottom. He presented the book, which read "Trees of the World."

"Thank you, sir," Mr. Jackson said.

"Put it on any of the carts when you're done." The man returned to his desk, stirring another spoonful of sugar into his cup before drinking his coffee.

Mr. Jackson found a table in view of the desk and sat to read.

"There you are." His wife sat across from him, setting a volume on the table.

Mr. Jackson glanced at the book, surprised. "I didn't know you'd read Emerson! I once knew a man who was a great admirer." The memory left him melancholy, so he focused again upon his page. "Did you know there are three trees at least called snake-wood? But one of them is where strychnine comes from."

Shock crossed his wife's face. "Really?"

"The seeds, apparently." He picked up another book he'd found called "Poisons from Plants," which unfortunately had no drawings or descriptions of the tree itself. "And they're devilishly hard seeds — very difficult to get the poison from." He considered the matter. "But that little thing planted in the hotel conservatory won't make seeds for twenty years, if what Albert Stayman says is true."

"Albert Stayman?"

"The husband of the dowager Duchess."

"Oh, yes," Mrs. Jackson said. "Now I remember. Does your book say anything else?"

Mr. Jackson shook his head. "Just a few lines. The book about the poisonous tree has been checked out." He sighed. "I suppose we'll have to wait until it's returned."

"That's quite a coincidence, isn't it?"

"That Mr. Stayman planted a snake-wood tree?" Mr. Jackson shrugged. "I'm not even sure the tree at the hotel is the poisonous kind." He thought about poisons for a moment. "But you can get strychnine at any grocery in the city. Sounds as if it'd be quicker just to go to the store and buy rat poison." He got up, went to the desk. "When will the book I wanted be returned?"

The man checked the file again. "Next week."

"Thanks, I'll come back then."

"Or I can get your number and call when it's here."

"Splendid!" Mr. Jackson gave him the number for the hotel. "Thanks ever so much."

His wife checked out the book she'd picked up and the couple went out to lunch. Afterward, they returned to the hotel for her pain medicine.

"I'll just take a drop," she said. "That way I won't sleep the rest of the day away."

A knock at the door, and Mr. Jackson went to answer it. A busboy stood there. "Good day, sir. The Myriad Hotel's owner, Mr. Montgomery Carlo, requests you and your wife dine with him at his residence this evening. A car will come for you at eight."

"Excellent! Please tell him we accept. Oh, and send up luncheon, if you will."

"Anything particular?"

"Whatever's good."

The busboy shrugged. "Hard to say, sir, now Cook's gone. They got a new lady in charge. I don't think she's nearly as good, but I'll do my best."

"Good man." Mr. Jackson gave him a tip and sent him on his way.

His wife fell asleep briefly, but woke when the food arrived a half hour later. The busboy was right: the food was merely adequate.

"I fear this hotel's reputation will suffer if they don't replace their cook with someone of equal caliber," Mr. Jackson said.

Mrs. Jackson snorted. "I wouldn't come back if they paid me, after having my name plastered in the papers so rudely."

"I hope for the Hotel's sake Miss Goldie Jean Dab has a more forgiving nature. Once we clear her name, that is."

"We must, if we're to stay here." She put down her fork. "I don't know if I want to stay somewhere with a poisoner in it for very long."

Mr. Jackson shook his head. "This feels too personal. I don't think we're in any danger. If it makes you feel better, I'll taste every dish before you eat it!"

She laughed at that. Then her face sobered. "I must sound like some anxious old woman."

"Surely not. You've had a difficult time." He pondered this a moment; when he glanced next at her, her eyes were red. He spoke gently, wondering what had upset her so. "But you're correct: we must find this killer, or we can't stay here for long." At that, he recalled George's reaction at the hospital, the way he'd suffered, and he leaned across the table to take her hand. "You wish to clear the cook's name, and to find whoever killed that young woman. I very much wish to stay here, and to find that poisoner for my own reasons. Shall we put aside our doubts and suspicions of the past and work together?"

14

His wife's eyes filled with tears, and she squeezed his hand tightly. "I'm sorry for how I've doubted you, so wrongly, over the years."

A pang of remorse. "Much of the fault was mine." He leaned over to kiss her hand. "I'm truly sorry for my part in it."

She rested her forehead on their hands, still joined. "How I wish I would have just spoken with you. So much hurt could have been avoided."

He smiled at her black curls, kissed them. "Don't berate yourself for the past. It's gone now."

She raised her head, dampness on her cheeks. "To answer your question: I can only promise to try."

Feeling a new energy, Mr. Jackson sat back. "There we have it!" He chuckled at the irony of the situation. "Now all we need to do is form some idea of how we might solve this."

"The killer is among us," Mrs. Jackson said, face pensive. "Right here, still, in the hotel. She holds such anger!"

"Yes," Mr. Jackson said, "and about something which likely happened long ago." He considered this. "Could the poisoner wish to frame the cook for some past slight?"

His wife shook her head. "For what, I have no idea." She let out a short laugh. "From your theory, we must know why first. But I disagree. We may never know why this woman does this, if it is indeed a woman at all. Knowing the facts of the matter will bring you to the answer."

He found this amusing. "Very well, Madam Investigator. What are the facts?"

His wife peered at him sideways. Then she chuckled. "I did sound rather imperious there." She began to tick off points on the fingers of her left hand. "There appear to be two kinds of death here. First is the young man, whose cause of death is still unknown. The second is two poisonings by strychnine." She paused, frowning. "Two murderers?"

"If the first was indeed murder."

"Yes," she said. "We still don't know if the deaths were related." She rubbed her left temple. "There's so much we don't yet know."

"There are still areas of the hotel yet unexplored, people yet to speak with." He considered this. "Every evening after tea, men gather in the barbershop downstairs. Perhaps one of them has seen something which may help."

Mrs. Jackson nodded. "The second point: so far as we know, all the poisonings have targeted the staff."

"And whoever should have gotten the lemon-cake with the bubble. Remember what George said? The cook noticed the bubble and switched the cakes."

His wife's eyes went wide. "I'd forgotten! Was there anyone of note in the list of room service calls that night?"

A shock ran through him. "The owner. He was here last night, in his room. Remember? We were supposed to meet with him after dinner."

Mrs. Jackson's eyes narrowed. "You suspected earlier that these poisonings were meant to discredit the hotel. What if this person actually targets the owner?"

"You mean that —"

"When the deaths didn't get the attention the poisoner wished, she decided to poison the owner directly."

Mr. Jackson leaned back. "Surely she didn't believe a few days' scandal would be sufficient to ruin a hotel of such magnificence? If so, this woman has clearly not thought the matter through."

His wife nodded. "A third point, then: the woman in question holds a quick and impulsive nature."

"But to plan this out, then change their tactics so suddenly?"

"Perhaps the poisoner doubted herself." She paused, her eyes far away. "It's easy to plan someone's death. The reality is often very different."

Mr. Jackson shuddered, remembering a scene of his own in which this was true. The memory left him feeling vaguely ill. "The swarm of police may have shaken the poisoner's resolve as well."

"Yes. To come so close to success ... then to see the police?" She shook her head. "It would take a will of steel to stand firm when your ultimate goal is endangered. It seems our killer is not such a person."

Mr. Jackson considered this for a moment and came up with exactly nothing. "I still have no idea what to do to find this woman. We need more information."

***

Mrs. Jackson put her sling on. "I shall go mad cooped up here much longer." The luncheon dishes lay upon their table waiting for the maids to return.

"Let's go for a stroll," Mr. Jackson said. Then he chuckled. "We shall have no madness here!"

She thought this quite amusing.

They left with the door sign turned to "Please clean room now" and descended to the lobby. As always, people bustled about in groups, gazed at the fine chandelier and the lovely fountain, chatted with friends.

The couple strolled through the vast lobby towards the front doors.

A middle-aged uniformed man at the valet stand turned his head towards them, frowning as he gazed downward.

A doorman opened the way for them, then also glanced down, moving his foot out. "Keep out, you!"

Mrs. Jackson looked down as well. A pair of liquid brown eyes encased in a mat of charcoal fur gazed hopefully up at her, its tail wagging a similar mat like a small flag. "What's this?"

"Just a stray, ma'am," the doorman said. "Been hanging about the past day or two."

Mrs. Jackson moved out of the doorway and knelt before the dog, whose feet and tail never stopped moving in its excitement. "Look how sweet its nature. This is someone's pet."

The dog hadn't stopped bounding up and down on its little legs, licking her hands, her face. She felt a collar under the thick mat. Twigs and leaves lay buried in the dog's fur.

People continued to pass in and out of the front doors, casting curious glances at her and the dog as they went.

Mr. Jackson knelt beside them. "They have a groomer here. Perhaps we —"

The man at the valet booth came over, frowning, and said to the doorman, "Is there a problem?"

To Mrs. Jackson's surprise, Mr. Jackson picked up the dog and rose. "Not at all." He grinned at her. "Let's see what's under all this nonsense, shall we?"

The groomer looked just as surprised when they brought the dog to him. "Looks like a sausage with legs!"

But after some dog food, a bowl of water, and an hour of clipping and coaxing, a rather thin toy poodle emerged. There was a ragged collar, sure enough, but any name-tag was long gone. Her skin was raw in spots, and the groomer gave them a salve to use for the next few days.

Mrs. Jackson looked into the little dog's eyes. "Where are your people?" She turned to Mr. Jackson and the groomer, "Someone is missing her dearly. How would we find her owner?"

The groomer shrugged. "She must have been on her own for a while, for all this to have grown and matted so. Maybe as long as a month."

Mr. Jackson said, "Do you have leashes for sale?"

"Why, yes," the groomer said. "There's a display case on the way in."

Moving out to the front area, they selected a fine black leather leash and a collar to match. Mr. Jackson said, "Would you bill our room?"

"Certainly, sir." The groomer handed over a slip of paper, which Mr. Jackson signed. "And if you need someone to walk her, just return here, or call down. My sons are available day and night, and we book appointments by the hour."

"Excellent!" Mr. Jackson put the dog down and handed her the leash. "Now, let's see where this little one takes us."

Freed from the constraints of matted fur, the little dog leaped and bounded back and forth, yet once out of the lobby, went right, then kept moving in a direct line.

"Go home," Mrs. Jackson said firmly. "Take us to your people."

The little dog began to pull on her leash with a purpose, and the couple followed several blocks before the dog pulled them to the right, across the busy street and down a tree-lined row of houses. A uniformed policeman stood outside one house, and the dog rushed up the steps towards him.

"Whoa," the policeman said to the trio. "You can't come in here. This is a crime scene."

Just then, Sergeant Nestor emerged, and which of them were the most surprised would be difficult to say.

The sergeant said, "Why are you here?"

Mrs. Jackson felt amused. "The dog brought us."

The sergeant's mouth dropped open, then he followed Mrs. Jackson's pointing hand to the dog and focused upon it for a good second. He put his hand to his forehead. "How did you find it?"

So they told the story of how the dog — more or less — found them. "We asked it to go home," Mr. Jackson said, "and here we are, it seems."

The dog pulled on its leash towards the open doorway. Mrs. Jackson, feeling compassion for the poor thing, picked it up. "Hush, there, little one." She felt sure the story the sergeant had to tell was an unhappy one. "We're here now."

Whether the dog understood Mrs. Jackson's words or not, it settled and became quiet.

The sergeant escorted them to the street. "The old lady was found dead inside. A few weeks is my guess. We saw the empty bowls yet no one knew where the dog went."

Mrs. Jackson felt shocked. "And the woman was just found now?"

"Last night," Sergeant Nestor said, wrinkling his nose. Then he focused on the dog. "You found it like this?"

Mr. Jackson said, "The poor thing was hungry, encased in a mat of fur." He shook his head in distaste.

"Had been nosing about the front of the hotel a day or two, perhaps looking for food, I don't know."

Mrs. Jackson said, "The poor little dear." Feeling a surge of compassion, she kissed the little dog's forehead. "So now what?"

The sergeant shrugged. "If you don't want the dog, we can —"

"I want it," Mrs. Jackson said. She glanced over at Mr. Jackson, who had a bemused smile on his lips. But he nodded, so she said, "We want it."

The sergeant chuckled. "I thought you might. Very well. If we need to ask anything —"

"You know where to find us," Mr. Jackson said. He tipped his fedora. "Good day, sergeant."

They returned to the hotel. Standing out on the sidewalk, Mrs. Jackson took the small dog in her hands, peering into its eyes. "This is home now." At that, she felt amused. "At least for now." She set the dog down; it went to the gutter to relieve itself.

Mrs. Jackson felt impressed. "You have good manners, at any rate."

Mr. Jackson stood watching. "What shall we call her?"

This brought back a fond memory: a small child on a large farm with a black cow. "Let's call her Bessie."

As she knew he would, Mr. Jackson laughed. "Bessie it is then!"

"Come on, Bessie," Mrs. Jackson said, and the little dog barked. "Let's show you your new home."

15

Bessie had great interest in sniffing every corner of the elevator, the hall, and most especially, their rooms.

"I hope the servants won't be too put out with her here," Mrs. Jackson said.

Mr. Jackson shrugged. "It's none of their affair. We'll keep her in the bathroom overnight, though, until we learn each others' ways."

Mrs. Jackson thought that a good plan. "We'll need food and water bowls. And a little bed."

Mr. Jackson chuckled. "I never knew you fancied animals so."

She'd never considered the matter before. "I suppose I do. I've always had animals of one kind or another." Looking at Bessie, she patted her knee. Bessie leaped onto her lap to snuggle there. For an instant, she was reminded of her little son, gone forever, and grief washed over her. "How cruel the world can be!"

"Yes," Mr. Jackson said, "but think of what might have happened had we come down a few moments later, and not been there to take her in."

At that, Mrs. Jackson hugged the little dog, grateful. Bessie was no replacement for the husband and son she'd lost forever, but with a dog's pure love, she was there.

***

The couple took tea in their rooms, just to let Bessie get used to them and her new surroundings.

They had some discussion about whether to bring Bessie with them to Mr. Carlo's home for dinner. Since Bessie had not been invited, they decided to leave her with the groomer's sons. The boys — ranging from ten to sixteen — instantly took to the little dog, with much fun being had on all sides.

The car which picked Mr and Mrs. Jackson up from the hotel was a marvel: expensive, with fine leather seats and gleaming brass fixtures. The driver, a middle-aged man with an impressive mustache, wore a black uniform with brass buttons, much as the door-men did.

Mrs. Jackson felt excited to finally meet the owner, yet had some trepidation. Why would this important man wish to meet them? She leaned over to speak in Mr. Jackson's ear. "What can you tell me about this man?"

Mr. Jackson shrugged. "Our meeting was quite brief. Perhaps I ought not cloud your perceptions with my own as yet."

Mrs. Jackson sighed, then nodded. She really wished to have some secure knowledge of what they walked into, yet his idea had merit. She settled in to view the scenery.

It appeared that Mr. Carlo lived in the countryside. The buildings and shops grew shorter, farther apart, and homes appeared. Trees lined the streets, and the lights came on. Finally, the car passed beside a tall fence of wrought iron to the right, and a grand mansion came into view, lit from above and below. They turned right. Men stood guard beside large gates, which opened, and the car drove down the fifty-yard drive past wide fields. Sheep grazed in the half-darkness.

White columns framed a wide overhang. The auto entered a circle and drove round to stop at the front door, which was painted red.

Men opened the doors for the couple, then escorted them up the steps and inside.

The owner, a stern-appearing man of middle age, came forward to greet them. A brown-haired woman — perhaps half his age — came up beside them.

Mrs. Jackson expected this to be his daughter, yet she was introduced as his wife Maisy.

"A pleasure to meet you both," Mr. Jackson said.

The brown-haired woman who'd sat next to Mrs. Jackson at breakfast at the hotel that first time was also there: Mr. Carlo's daughter Margaret. All around came the refrain: "What a surprise to see you!"

The dinner was excellent: a salad with walnuts and apples, roasted pheasant, creamed potatoes with rosemary, with a sweet rice pudding and biscotti.

After dinner, the group moved to the parlor. Mr. Carlo and his family drank as if it were not forbidden to them by law, which amused Mrs. Jackson no end. Finally, the younger couple took their leave for bed. "We have an early start tomorrow."

Mr. and Mrs. Jackson also rose.

"Oh, don't leave on our account," Margaret said. "Visit with my parents as long as you like."

"Please stay," said Maisy, and her husband agreed, so they did.

Mrs. Jackson still wasn't sure why they'd been invited. "To what do we owe the honor of your invitation?"

Maisy Carlo smiled. "We've so wanted to meet you, but especially after you rescued George."

Mrs. Jackson felt perplexed.

"The waiter you saved from the poison," Mr. Carlo said. "My wife's cousin."

"Ah," Mr. Jackson said. "A fine young man."

"He is," Mr. Carlo said. "I admire his desire to make his own way, rather than live idly on his family's money." The man nodded. "Good spirit, that."

"Thank you so much for visiting him," Maisy said. "We all appreciate your kindness." She seemed sweet and gentle enough, but a glint of steel lay in her eyes. "Truly we mean to have this poisoner pay for her outrage."

"This is something I meant to speak about, if it wouldn't offend," Mr. Jackson said.

Mr. Carlo leaned back, and became very still, his gaze hooded. "The sergeant told me of your assessment."

Maisy looked back and forth between them. "What?"

Mr. Carlo said, "It's nothing, my dear."

"Mrs. Carlo," Mrs. Jackson said, "we believe the cook to be innocent of these crimes."

Maisy Carlo turned to her husband. "Monty, what's going on?"

Mr. Carlo didn't look happy. "Madam, I'd rather you hadn't told her that."

"Why? She's a grown woman. She deserves the truth. I said as much to your cousin's father, and he dismissed it out of hand. But I tell you," she pointed at Mr. Carlo, "there's sure to be more murders. And I believe whoever it is targets you."

The man raised an eyebrow. "Me? Whatever for?"

"I have no idea," Mr. Jackson said. "But last night's poisoned lemon-cake may have been meant for you."

Maisy Carlo gasped. "Well, then, you must find this killer!"

Mr. Jackson's shoulders slumped. "The police have forbidden us to do any real investigation. I've spoken with some of the staff, at your manager's request, but —"

"Continue to do so," Mr. Carlo said. He stood, went to a set of cabinets, where he took a pad and wrote upon it. He folded the paper in half and handed it to Mr. Jackson. "Call me if you need anything."

It seemed then — just like that — the visit was over.

***

The couple had never used their parlor as yet, but it had the largest table. Once they returned to their suite, Mr. Jackson went to walk Bessie. On his return, he found that his wife had collected stationery, note pads, and fountain pens from every room. Lists were placed at intervals along the table, with the pens standing in a water glass in the center.

Dismayed, Mr. Jackson watched her write another list. "Doesn't all that writing hurt your arm?"

She shrugged. "If it gets too painful, I'll take my medication and go to bed."

"But the doctor said you needed rest."

She set the pen down. "I fail to see how that's your concern."

"All I care about is your welfare." Mr. Jackson said. "What if you re-injured it? For all you know, you may be prolonging the process."

She gave him a piercing glance, full of doubt, hope.

She still doesn't trust me.

"This is what we know about the first death," she muttered. Her black and brass pen flashed reflections from the lamp as the pad jostled it. "He lay facing towards us, cup in hand. Yet the cup had not one drop in it."

Across the room, Mr. Jackson leaned back in his overstuffed chair, seeing nothing but his own remorse at how he'd hurt her. "Perhaps he'd just washed it, and liked to keep it at his post." He pictured the scene. "Perhaps he sensed he was dying, and tried to get help, without even time to lay the cup aside."

His wife's eyes turned red, and he instantly regretted speaking. "Forgive me."

She let out a soft snort, smiling to herself. "For inspiring me to compassion?" She sat staring at the table.

He didn't know how to reply. She'd said nothing of what happened the night before they wed. He knew the outcome, of course, but not how or why. Until now, he'd thought it best to let her speak of it when she was ready.

"For all my life, I've been a hard woman. Focused, driven. And everyone around me has paid for my pursuit." She raised her eyes to his. "It's likely that more compassion is what I need."

He leaned forward, feeling uneasy. "First have compassion on yourself! What's likely is that the police will find this killer, or if not, perhaps I will. In any case, you're allowed to rest, to enjoy safety. To let yourself heal." He let out a bitter laugh. "You don't need to save everyone."

Her gaze dropped. "I remember telling my husband that once." She shook her head, her eyes reddening once more.

He moved to sit on her left side. "I know I can never replace him. Or your son." He felt lost. "I don't even know where to start."

"You don't have to." She grasped his hand tightly. "Don't give up on me."

A laugh burst from him. "All I ask is the same." He enveloped her in an embrace, kissed her hair. "How did we — of all people — end up **here**?"

Her arm moved warm around his waist, and when she spoke, he heard the smile. "You know as much as anyone."

16

After his wife left for her bed, Mr. Jackson lay upon his, feeling drained yet unable to sleep. How was he to find this murderess?

It seemed all he could do to protect his wife and keep her from harm.

He'd told the sergeant he'd been a private investigator, but amateur was too strong a word for it.

I don't know what I'm doing.

He didn't know what he was doing, in either this investigation or this marriage. Yet in the past he'd always had friends, family to rely on. To ask for advice and help.

Albert Stayman and the dowager Duchess seemed happy in their marriage. While they'd be no help with investigating a murder, perhaps they might be able to give advice on other matters.

***

Early the next morning, Mr. Jackson left his wife sleeping, a note on the table as to where he'd gone, and went to the gardens.

He found Albert Stayman slowly sweeping the stone walkway beside the pond.

"My gracious me!" Albert seemed astonished. "How grand to see you here!"

"I did say I might visit," Mr. Jackson said. "And I thought you might be here now. I'm glad you're feeling improved."

The old man gazed over the water. "My favorite time of day."

He followed Albert's gaze. Toads croaked, small birds chirped, and the water gurgled along. "It's quite peaceful."

Albert smiled to himself, scooping up his pile of leaves, which he deposited off of the path with trembling hands. "First spat?"

"What? No, I mean, not the first. But how did you know?"

"Cordelia saw your lights on late when she got in. Couple on their honeymoon wouldn't have reason for lights that late unless they were set to discussion." He winked. "Then here you are." He rubbed the back of his neck. "Only been married the once, and not yet four years at that." He shrugged. "But I'm glad you came by."

What could he say which wouldn't reveal too much? "Well, my wife's a widow, and —"

Albert nodded. "I see." He let out a breath. "I remember how Cordelia cried, after he passed. About broke my heart." He bit his upper lip, nose reddening. "It's a difficult matter, coming after a marriage, even when she loves you. As she said it, nothing's the same. For a while it seems she'll never be happy again. And you love her, so you'll do anything to make it right. But you don't know what, or how."

Mr. Jackson felt unsure right then which of them Albert referred to.

Albert glanced up and sniffled. He got out his handkerchief. "I'll have Cordelia talk to your wife, see what she can do."

"I'd be much obliged, sir."

Albert laughed. "Don't 'sir' me. Makes me sound old and much more important than I am. Please, call me Albert."

"All right, Albert. And I'm —" It'd been years since he'd said it, but all of a sudden he came too close to giving his real name. "Hector."

Albert gave him an amused smile. "Pleasure's all mine. Come on, let's find some flowers for our young ladies."

***

Mrs. Jackson woke at a knock on the door. She struggled into a robe and answered it: Mrs. Knight stood there.

The lady's maid bustled in. "Good morning to you! Did you sleep well?"

"I did. What time is it?"

"Nine, ma'am."

"Oh! Well," at this, she laughed at herself. "I suppose we best get started."

Her arm ached from her writing exertions the night prior, and as she soaked in the hot water, she considered what Mr. Jackson had said. *You don't need to save everyone.*

"It's twenty to ten," Mrs. Knight said.

She felt amused by this. "Up I go then." She rose, took the towel the maid held up for her. On the side of the maid's right thumb lay a pale patch of skin, which reminded Mrs. Jackson of the young dead man's face. "What's happened there?"

The maid let out a short laugh. "My daughter's got this new cream for clearing the skin. Asked me to put it on her. I used gloves, but it must have soaked through there."

"My word," Mrs. Jackson said. "What sort of cream is it?"

"For blemishes," the maid said. "I might have it in my purse here." She left for the other room, returning with a small metal tube, which read, "Doctor Smith's Facial Brightening Cream." She handed it to Mrs. Jackson, saying, "My daughter says it's all the rage these days. You know how kids are. They constantly say, 'All the young people are doing it,' as if that means it's safe. I didn't want her to use it until I'd investigated, but apparently it's true. Makes your skin ghastly pale for a day, then it peels, and your skin is ever so much clearer." She chuckled. "Only problem is you look ghastly pale for a day, then your face peels. Most people take a few days off work."

Mrs. Jackson turned it over, where it read, "Contains Phenol". She let out a laugh. "So that's what I smelled!"

"Smelled, ma'am?"

She recalled a sick room, long ago. "Oh, nothing. Just talking to myself." She felt happy to have solved this particular mystery!

***

Mr. Jackson hurried upstairs to ready himself for the day, a bouquet of azalea blossoms in hand. His valet stood waiting.

As Mr. Jackson was being dressed, Mr. Vienna said, "There's not time to shave you before breakfast, sir. I have another appointment across town at half past ten."

Mr. Jackson shrugged. "No matter. One day shouldn't make a difference."

Mr. Vienna helped him into his jacket. "Sir, I did want to speak with you briefly on a private matter."

Mr. Jackson felt surprised. "How may I help?"

Mr. Vienna seemed hesitant. "Well, sir, I've asked my sweetheart to marry me."

"Congratulations! Will you need time off so soon?"

Relief passed over the man's face. "It's just — I mean — I thought you might be angry, sir."

Mr. Jackson chuckled to himself. "Not at all. You're a fine young man, and I wish you the best."

"Thank you, sir."

"What will you do once you're married?"

"Oh, I'll continue with the agency."

"Splendid! We should be here at least a week longer, I'd think, then we might take a trip abroad. But when we return, I'll ask for you."

A soft knock. Mr. Vienna extended his hand with a real smile. "Thank you very much, sir." He went to the parlor door, opened it.

Mrs. Jackson stood there. "Sorry to intrude."

"No, not at all," Mr. Jackson said. He took up the bouquet. "For you."

"How lovely!" His wife rushed out with the flowers.

"I'll be leaving now, sir," Mr. Vienna said.

"And I'll see you this evening?"

"Of course, sir."

Mr. Jackson went into the parlor, where the flowers stood, his wife having pressed a water carafe into use as a vase. "Where would you like to have breakfast today?"

"Let's go down to the dining room," his wife said. "Perhaps this new cook is better at breakfast than luncheon."

So the couple went down to eat. The dining room was only half as full as it had been the first day they arrived, and very few new faces lay among those there. As Mr. Jackson sat with his wife to wait for their meals, he considered of the conversation he'd just had with his valet. How long had the young man worried over what he might say? Did he fear being given a bad report, or even fired?

How difficult the life of a servant must be, he thought.

But Mr. Jackson felt quite pleased when his wife gave him the news about the facial cream. "So that's why the man's face was so pale. How extraordinary! But how appalling! Your face **peels**? And people actually **use** this?"

"They do. Apparently it's quite well known."

He shook his head. "What people will do for appearances."

She let out an ironic laugh, and he grinned at her.

The stout little maid, Maria, who'd found the first man's body when they arrived, came to the table. "Care for something to drink?"

"Just water, thanks," Mrs. Jackson said.

"Coffee with heavy cream, no sugar," said Mr. Jackson.

"Right away," Maria said, disappearing into the crowd.

Just then, the doors opened and the clerk he'd met earlier came in. "A message for you, sir," he said, handing over a slip of paper.

Mr. Jackson took the slip from him, got out a tip. "Mr. Francis, is it not?"

The man beamed. "It is, sir, thank you."

"Give my regards to your wife."

"Yes, sir. I will, sir." The man hurried off.

Mr. Jackson unfolded the note: the librarian reported that the book had been returned early, and could be picked up at his convenience. "Wonderful!"

Mrs. Jackson said, "A new clue to report?"

"Not particularly." He handed over the slip for her to read. "But it just occurred to me that the back entry to the kitchens has no door."

"Is that so?"

"Indeed. Anyone could simply walk in." He considered this for a moment. "In fact, they wouldn't even have to enter the building through the front door. The exit to the dock lies not ten yards away."

"That's disturbing. I wonder if the good sergeant has put a guard there."

"Hmm," Mr. Jackson said. "It's likely he did. But I'll take a look later on."

"Good thinking. No need to stir that hornet's Nest- or —"

At that, he laughed.

"- unless need be."

"You are incorrigible," he said, quite amused at the comparison.

The dowager Duchess and her husband came to the table. "It's so good to see you smiling," Cordelia said.

Mr. Jackson stood. "Please join us!"

Mrs. Jackson said, "Why smiling?"

Cordelia sat beside her. "My dear, dear girl. Your Mr. Jackson told my Albert about your predicament —"

Mrs. Jackson turned to Mr. Jackson, face alarmed.

"Now, now," the dowager said. She lowered her voice. "He merely told him you'd been widowed. As I was widowed myself, I completely sympathize."

From the set of her jaw, Mr. Jackson felt certain his wife would have words with him later on. "It's true," she said. "But —"

The dowager patted Mrs. Jackson's hand. "Nothing more need be said." Her tone turned bright. "After breakfast, would you like to sit with me here in the library? We can find a nice corner where no one will be bothered by our clucking."

Mr. Jackson tried very hard not to laugh at the look which crossed his wife's face. Being compared to a chicken did not amuse her in the slightest.

"Very well," she said. "I did want to spend time there. Reading."

"Well, my dear, we can do whatever you prefer," the dowager said. "I don't want to be a bother. I just know how hard it is to lose a husband."

Mrs. Jackson nodded, eyes on the tablecloth.

"Well, that's perfect," Mr. Jackson said. "You'll be entertained while I'm off to the Main Library." He brandished the slip, then turned to Cordelia. "A book I very much wanted to read has come in."

"Your drinks," the maid Maria said, placing them.

Albert said, "Which book?"

"You might like it as well," he said. "It's the only one they have on the snake-wood tree. Want me to check it out and bring it by once I'm done reading?"

"That won't be necessary," Albert said. "I've read it before."

Maria turned to Albert and Cordelia. "What would you like?"

"Tea with lemon for us both," Albert said. "Steep it well."

"Yes, sir, I remember," she said in reply, but as if she'd said so a dozen times already.

"We're ready for our meals," Mr. Jackson said.

"Right away, sir."

It seemed Maria was the only one taking care of the huge room, and it was some time before their meals arrived. "So sorry for the wait. We're short on staff today."

Mr. Jackson said, "I hope no one's ill."

"No, sir. Today's the funeral for the two who passed away. Miss Agnes and ... that new man. I've forgotten his name."

Dismay crossed Albert's face. "That's today? Right now?"

"At noon, sir. Trips Cemetery."

Mr. Jackson said, "Does the girl have family?"

Maria shook her head. "Just us at the hotel." She glanced towards the room. "Enjoy your meal."

She moved off, but Albert rose. "Wait!"

"Now, Bertie," Cordelia said. "Let the woman get to her work!"

The maid returned. "Is something wrong?"

"Who's taking care of the expenses?"

"The owner —"

Albert flinched, and his jaw tightened.

"He's offered a back room for lunch afterward." She glanced behind her. "Please excuse me."

Mr. Jackson recalled what the dowager had said about Albert employing the young woman for errands. "Did you know her well?"

Albert said, "What? No. Not really."

They ate in silence. A woman shouted from far off, and pots clattered.

All the while, Albert picked at his food.

Mr. Jackson said, "Is something amiss, sir?"

Albert said, "What? No."

Why was Albert so cross all of a sudden? "It seems kind of the owner to foot the bill for his employees' funerals."

Albert scowled.

Cordelia patted Albert's hand. "Monty's a good man, once you get to know him."

"Oh," Mr. Jackson said, "you know Mr. Carlo well, then?"

"He's her former brother-in-law," Albert said sourly. "Husband's sister's husband. That is, until he ran off with that girl. Not much older than his daughter!"

"Bertie!" Cordelia looked horrified. "I know you two don't get along, but you shouldn't speak of such things in public." She turned to Mrs. Jackson. "They were so unhappy — it doesn't surprise me that —"

Albert drained his teacup and rose, leaving his plate half full. "I have errands to run."

Cordelia blinked. "You do?"

"I'll be back shortly." He turned to Mr. Jackson. "Enjoy your book."

Cordelia frowned as he went off. Then she sighed. "He was ever so fond of Agnes. I bet he's gone to cut flowers for her grave."

"Perhaps so," Mr. Jackson said. Yet he felt something more was going on.

"I'm going up to get my shawl," Cordelia said to Mrs. Jackson. "Would you like to meet in the library?"

"That would be fine, thank you." Once she'd left, Mrs. Jackson said, "Why did you tell her I was a widow?"

He looked at her, feeling sad.

Her eyes reddened. "I know I am. A widow. But this is the second time you've told them things about me. You didn't even ask! I know you like them, but can we trust them? The woman's mouth runs on about anything. If she tells the wrong person something —"

He put his hand on hers. "What might she tell? That you're a widow? That I saw your legs once?"

At that, she went crimson.

"Look at me."

She turned to meet his gaze, chin held high, defiant tears in her eyes.

"All will be well." He felt compassion, and resolve. "Don't be afraid. What I told you on the way here, I meant. Literally. I would give my life before I let anyone harm you."

Her shoulders slumped, then she glanced at Albert's plate. "The meal wasn't so bad as all that."

Perhaps it wasn't acceptance, but it was enough. "Something troubles him, that's clear. I suppose he'll tell us when he's ready." He leaned over to kiss her cheek.

"Let me collect this book, then I'll look behind the kitchens."

He could tell she'd forgotten by the way her face changed. "Oh! Yes. I'm glad you remembered!" She chuckled, wiped her eyes with her napkin. "Hopefully everything will be in order."

"I do hope so, for all our sakes."

***

Mr. Jackson caught a cab to the Main Library. As it was well after eleven, the streets were busy. The day was breezy and bright, perfect for an outing.

He still didn't know how they were going to find this killer, but for a moment, it didn't matter. The police were ever so busily on the case, and his wife would be in the hotel's library with the dowager Duchess, as safe as she might be anywhere. Surely a short detour to read a book for pleasure's sake wouldn't hurt anything.

As Mr. Jackson climbed the steps to the Library, he thought: Albert was right. What Mrs. Jackson needed was a kindly, sympathetic ear, which Duchess Cordelia Stayman could certainly provide.

Mr. Jackson felt glad they'd found friends here. The dowager Duchess was a bit nosy and at times lacked tact, but he enjoyed being with Albert. The old couple could show them around the city once his wife was well enough.

And he hoped once young waiter George was well, they could go boating together — with his wife, of course. It wouldn't be quite proper otherwise, under the circumstances.

But did she like boats? He didn't even know.

It'd been a while since he'd sailed the river in his yacht back home. Of course, his men were caring for the boat, but it was unlikely he'd ever sail it again. Perhaps his sister might like it.

Yes, he decided. He'd give it to her, the next time he wrote.

He went through the enormous main hall and up a small flight of wide steps to the non-fiction section. A crowd of people milled around up ahead near the Natural History desk, and as he approached, he saw the uniforms of police. Men carried away a body covered in linen.

Mr. Jackson hurried to the desk, alarmed. "What happened?"

Sergeant Nestor turned to face him, then frowned. "You again." He gestured at the body with his chin. "The librarian's dead."

17

Mr. Jackson leaned on the desk, feeling unsteady. "Dead? How?"

"The same as the rest, sir. Poison."

For a moment, Mr. Jackson was too astonished to speak. "This is incredible."

The sergeant peered at him. "What are you doing here?"

He felt as if in a fog. The man had just been alive! "I — I got a message from him. The librarian. My book was ready."

Sergeant Nestor grabbed his arm. "Let's sit down."

Mr. Jackson was led to the very table where he'd sat during his last visit. "It doesn't seem possible. How could this be? Who would kill a librarian?"

The sergeant's eyes narrowed. "Who knew you were coming here?"

"Um ... the desk clerk. What was —? Oh, yes. Lee Francis was his name. He took the message. Then, let's see. The dowager Duchess and her husband were having breakfast with me and my wife." He glanced at the sergeant. "I mentioned it to them. I don't know who else." His head felt all a mush, and he rubbed his temples. "A maid waited on us — Maria — the same one who found the first body!" Could she have done this? "Perhaps she overheard us, I don't recall." He tried to focus. "I'm sorry. I can't think of who else might have known."

"What book were you here for?"

"A book about the snake-wood tree."

The sergeant laughed. "A whole book about a **tree**?"

Mr. Jackson shrugged. "One's growing in the Hotel gardens. A tree, not a book." He felt flustered, tried to collect himself. "I think it's the same one. Same tree, I mean. The book would have told me for sure. The book's about the tree that makes strychnine."

That got the sergeant's attention. "Is it now?"

"Well, not that little tree — I guess it takes twenty years or so to get the seeds. If it's the same tree. That's where the poison is."

"Didn't that strike you as odd, though?"

"I suppose. But I read that the seeds are incredibly hard and tough, so it takes a great deal of effort to grind them. It seemed to me that it would be easier to just buy some strychnine at the grocery. If you wanted to kill someone, that is."

"And did you want to kill someone?"

Mr. Jackson stared at the sergeant, shocked. "Of course not! What kind of man do you take me for?"

Sergeant Nestor let out a sigh. "The common factor in three murders and one attempted murder has been you. I don't know if you're doing it, or if it's possible someone's trying to frame you. But you have to admit it's disturbing."

A laugh burst from Mr. Jackson at the absurdity. Then he sobered. "Well, yes, you're right — it's quite disturbing." Especially the idea that someone might be doing all this to frame him. No one of any real importance knew he was even here. "Who'd want to frame me for murder?"

"You got me on that one." Then his eyes narrowed. "I still don't know who you even are."

Mr. Jackson raised an eyebrow. "I recall telling you all about myself."

"You're on your honeymoon, you're rich, and you arrived the morning of the first murder. But from where?"

"You never asked! Do you want my ticket stubs? My itinerary? I've been to a dozen cities in the past month. As I told you, my business takes me all over the country."

"I want you to level with me."

"I have. I've answered all of your questions. My property holdings here in Chicago are public record. I'm not sure what else you want me to say." He felt more than a bit annoyed at this man. "Am I under arrest?"

"No."

"Then I'll get my book and go."

But when they searched for the book, and the card on file listing who had it before this, both were gone.

***

When Mr. Jackson returned to the hotel, reporters were everywhere. Yet his wife and the dowager Duchess weren't in the library.

He went to the front desk, where Mr. Lee Francis still stood. "Have you by any chance seen my wife?"

"I imagine she's up with the Duchess, sir."

"In her rooms?"

"Yes." He shook his head. "Terrible thing to happen."

Alarmed, Mr. Jackson said, "What happened?"

"Someone's attacked the Duchess!"

Mr. Jackson stared at the young man, horrified, then dashed for the elevators.

The wait seemed interminable, and he pushed his way in. "Thirty-two, please."

The elevator seemed to take forever to climb, and every time it stopped his dread mounted.

Who would attack Cordelia Stayman? Was this related, or was it a coincidence? Had his wife been with the Duchess during the attack, and if so, had she been harmed? If a Duchess wasn't safe, were they safe here?

Finally, the elevator opened, and he ran to Albert and Cordelia's suite. Uniformed police stood in the hall, yet let him pass without so much as a glance.

Duchess Cordelia lay upon a sofa in her parlor, a pack of ice on her right temple. Albert sat beside her, holding her hand, while Mrs. Jackson stood pacing the room.

When Mr. Jackson entered, out of breath, his wife rushed to him. "You're here at last!"

He held her in his arms. "I came as soon as I heard." He squeezed her tightly, heart pounding, eyes stinging. Then he let go, grasped her arms. "How could such a thing happen?"

His wife shook her head. "I went to the library and she wasn't there. I waited quite some time, then came up here. Mr. Stayman had found her on the floor," she pointed to a spot by the coffee table.

She lowered her voice to a whisper. "Poor man was so upset he couldn't think straight. He didn't want any scandal, and she kept insisting she was fine. But a woman of her age suffering a blow to the head? A robber in the hotel? I called for the police and a doctor straightaway."

"You did exactly right." He turned towards Cordelia, trying to consider what best to say. He finally settled on, "How are you?"

The dowager chuckled. "As well as can be expected. And before you ask, a man was in my suite. I didn't see him — he pushed past from behind and knocked me down." She considered this. "I must have hit my head on the table; the next thing I remember is Bertie putting me on the sofa." She rubbed her husband's hand with her thumb and smiled up at him.

Albert's face was set in stone, wet with tears. "I almost **lost** you through my foolishness!"

"Oh, Bertie," she said, "flowers for a grave is never foolishness. Besides, nothing like this has ever happened before! How could you have expected it?" She pressed his hand to her cheek. "You mustn't blame yourself."

Mr. Jackson turned to his wife. "And the doctor?"

"Come and gone. He said we must keep watch over her, but he'll be back in an hour or so."

It was then Mr. Jackson noticed an empty spot on the bookcase. "Was anything taken?"

Albert looked dazed. "I don't believe so." He turned back to Cordelia. "Perhaps she surprised him before he might make off with anything."

"We don't have much worth taking," Cordelia said. "Everything was sold with the estate when my first husband died." A hint of sadness crossed her face. "Most of the jewels. What I have might fetch a few hundred dollars, that's all."

Mr. Jackson said, "What do the police say?"

He heard Sergeant Nestor's tread before the man spoke. "I say, Mr. Jackson, that you do get around."

18

Mrs. Jackson felt horrified. "What's this about?"

Mr. Jackson turned to her. "This man," he said, pointing at the sergeant, "believes I am the — how did you put it? The 'common factor' in three murders and one attempted. And, I suppose now, this assault?"

"That's absurd," Albert said. "Why would anyone blame him for this? He wasn't even here when it happened."

Mrs. Jackson felt confused. "Three murders?"

That was how she learned of the librarian's death.

It frightened her. Could someone know they were here and be trying to bring their presence to the attention of the law without the two of them knowing? They were doing a fine job of it. She turned to the sergeant. "Is that really what you think? Or is this some play to see what we'll do?"

Sergeant Nestor's face hardened. "I need to solve these cases! And as yet, we have no real idea who's doing them."

Mrs. Jackson felt bitter. "And yet you hold an innocent woman behind bars."

Albert flinched.

"That said," Sergeant Nestor replied, "we have no proof she didn't do the poisonings in the hotel, and a great deal of evidence she did." He glanced at Mr. Jackson, then back at her. "Since the two of you feel compelled to insert yourselves into this investigation, I'll tell you. Lunches are provided as an employee benefit. They're set up each day by the Hotel under the direction of the cook. Each lunch-box is labeled with the employee's name, so someone wishing to kill a particular person had the exact means to do so. On the day the young woman died, one person's lunch had an icing on the dessert that the others did not. Can you guess what was in that icing?"

Mrs. Jackson gasped in horror.

Albert pressed his face into the cushions beside Cordelia.

Mr. Jackson said, "So the target **was** the young woman." He turned away, shaking his head. "I suppose that unless we catch this killer, we'll never know how she offended him. Or her."

Mrs. Jackson blurted out, "Who would want to kill a young woman? This is monstrous!"

Without turning from the cushions, Albert snapped, "Would you take this discussion elsewhere? My wife needs her rest!"

Sergeant Nestor said, "Of course, sir, you're absolutely right. My apologies."

The three of them went into the hall.

Mrs. Jackson leaned against the wall, eyes closed. How could they possibly find this killer? They had so little information to go on. Yet it would be wrong to sit idly by while people died around them.

She felt weary, and her arm ached. She'd need her medication soon.

A hand rested on her shoulder; on opening her eyes, she saw it belonged to Mr. Jackson. His dark eyes looked concerned, and she smiled at him. "I'm just tired."

Sergeant Nestor stood peering at them both. "Perhaps we might go to your suite, sir. Then we can continue this discussion while your wife rests."

The relief on Mr. Jackson's face touched her, and she clasped his hand, feeling a surge of emotion. He cared about her, more than just any promises he'd made. Why, she didn't know, the story of her legs notwithstanding, but that didn't matter. More than anything, she wanted to be safe, with someone she could trust, at least until she got well.

And he wanted to take care of her.

Perhaps she'd made the right decision to let this man into her life.

***

As they walked to their suite, Mr. Jackson considered what the sergeant had told them. Not only that, how he'd told them, in front of the old couple.

Once he got his wife settled in her room, he went back to the parlor, where Sergeant Nestor still stood. "What aren't you telling us?"

The sergeant gave him a quick glance. "You're good, I'll grant you that. Sit down."

So he sat, wondering what could have possibly happened that the sergeant couldn't just come out and say. Bessie trotted over, curled up at his feet.

Sergeant Nestor settled himself upon the sofa. "The first rule — well, a first rule — of homicide is that the prime suspects come from those who 'find' the body. So of course, I suspected you two at once."

Mr. Jackson nodded. That seemed fair.

"Especially when you inserted yourselves into the investigation." He glanced aside, then back. "But you've never acted like suspects. You've volunteered information which killers wouldn't want known. You've shown concern for the victims. It's become clear to me that you're trying to solve these cases," he let out a short laugh, "whatever your reasons, rather than perpetrate them."

171

This surprised Mr. Jackson. "I'm glad of that."

The sergeant peered at him. "Besides, it's unlikely you managed to appear in two places at once."

"Sir?"

"The interesting thing about strychnine is that while it acts quickly, it doesn't act instantly. The body must take it in first. So we have a fairly precise time of action for each poisoning. You were in a taxi at the time of the first death, seen walking the park with your wife at the time of the second. You and your wife were at dinner when the waiter was poisoned. You and your wife were seen at breakfast by numerous people when the librarian was poisoned. And you were with me when Duchess Stayman was attacked."

Mr. Jackson chuckled. "There is that." He remembered something. "Do you have the back way into the kitchens guarded?"

"Of course."

"Good." Mr. Jackson felt relieved. Then he felt startled. "The first death, you say. Have you learned the cause of it?"

The sergeant shook his head. "Only that it wasn't strychnine. The man's stomach was completely empty, and no signs of poison were in his body."

This was an entire surprise. "So what caused it?"

Sergeant Nestor shrugged. "The coroner is as puzzled as anyone. He's doing another, more detailed autopsy. But the rest surely are related." He hesitated, just an instant. "You asked several very good questions back in the dowager's suite. What you don't know is that the young lady's lunch wasn't poisoned."

Mr. Jackson peered at the sergeant, trying to understand. "It wasn't?"

"Nope," the sergeant said. "The one being poisoned — who you saved, by the way — was the manager."

***

Sergeant Nestor watched as Mr. Jackson's face went from confusion to astonishment. Unless he was a better actor than any other, it seemed unlikely this man had anything to do with the poisonings.

The coroner was convinced the poisonings were related — the man had tried to explain the science of it to him, but Sergeant Nestor didn't really understand. What mattered was that someone was poisoning people in his precinct, and he wasn't going to stand for it. He no longer believed this Jackson fellow was involved. Yet somehow, the man kept coming to the center of it all.

But how much to reveal? Sergeant Nestor honestly had no idea who was perpetrating these crimes — if they were indeed related. And he couldn't keep the cook in jail forever. Her family had hired a lawyer, and were threatening to go to the papers if they didn't either release her or show proof of her guilt.

Sergeant Nestor had never accepted unqualified civilians onto an investigation. Not only did it put them at risk, it made it near impossible to convict later on. He'd heard horror tales of rules broken, evidence damaged, chain of custody ruined.

But these people seemed determined to assist, and if he didn't at least let them think they were, they were likely to ruin things. "I'll allow you to help. But it's going to be done my way. And you're going to — right now — tell me everything you know about these murders."

While he was speaking the last sentence, something changed in the man's face. He knew something, but not about the murders. Something else was going on that he hesitated to share. "Look, I'm not interested in your personal life, or whatever nonsense is going on in the hotel, unless it has to do with these murders! But let me be the judge of that."

The man gave him an odd glance — deciding whether to talk, perhaps — then he relaxed. "Very well, then."

In truth, it was a sad story. Mr. Jackson's closest friend (but not lover — the man was horrified at the idea) was in love with a woman not his.

On his deathbed, the friend made Mr. Jackson take a vow to care for the woman he loved. When the woman became a widow, Mr. Jackson found that the only way to keep his vow was to marry her himself. They arrived here, found the body. The rest seemed a curious chain of events, the two blundering into one crime scene after another.

It explained much. "What do you think of this latest death?"

For an instant, Mr. Jackson seemed confused. Then he said, "The librarian."

"Yes."

"If it's not related, it seems a terrible coincidence." A knock at the door, and Mr. Jackson went to open it. "Yes, he's here. I'll give it to him."

Sergeant Nestor took the slip of paper from Mr. Jackson's hand and read it. "I don't believe in coincidence." He held up the paper. "The old lady we found dead, the one this dog belonged to? We've finally identified a next of kin. Not that it'll help much."

"What do you mean?"

"She was our dead maid's grandmother."

***

Mr. Jackson looked down at his wife's dog, who now nestled in his lap. "Today is full of revelations."

"Indeed," Sergeant Nestor said. Then he rose. "May I use your phone?"

Mr. Jackson gestured towards where it sat on its stand. "I insist."

While the sergeant got connected to whoever he called, Mr. Jackson pondered the news. How was this old woman's death related? It happened weeks ago.

"Yeah, get them both up here," Sergeant Nestor said. "3205, parlor door. And bring a portrait of the old lady with you." He put down the phone.

The dog began to whine, and Mr. Jackson called down for someone to walk her.

Soon after little Bessie trotted off with the groomer's boy, the others arrived: an officer with the old woman's portrait, the stern head valet, and the manager.

"Yeah, I remember her," the valet said. "Walked down here almost every day for a while. I wondered why the dog seemed familiar."

Mr. Davis, the manager, didn't remember her. "Was it about an application?"

"No," Sergeant Nestor said, "she was the grandmother of the young lady. Miss Agnes."

"Oh! Well, I don't deal with family. Shouldn't have been allowed to visit the girl at work in the first place. If she'd been coming down here, I wouldn't know of it."

So they all went down to see the desk clerk. Mr. Lee Francis was fortunately still at his post, as he'd been here as long as any. "I do remember her. Not right in the head; would tell me the same story every day." He frowned. "She's not been by for weeks now."

When told she'd been found dead, he appeared shocked. Even more so when he learned she was the young lady's grandmother. "But she never asked for Agnes — she'd just come by. Been coming by for years now, every day at the same time like clockwork. How strange."

Sergeant Nestor said, "What story did she tell?"

"About some plant that would kill you. She said even the bark would kill you. 'Stop your heart dead,' she said." He laughed. "It was strange, but every hotel's got a story like that. The things my buddies tell me about!" He stopped then, sobered. "Then one day she quit coming. I didn't think anything of it until a few days later. I asked, but no one knew where she lived."

"Now that is strange," Sergeant Nestor said. "And you're sure she never mentioned Agnes?"

"She never asked for anyone. She'd just come up and start talking. Then when she was done, she'd leave."

A line was forming, presumably people waiting to check into the hotel. "Very well," Sergeant Nestor said. "I'll let you get back to work." So everyone left.

But Mr. Jackson thought this sounded too much the coincidence. So he waited.

Finally, the clerk had a moment. "Did you need something, sir?"

Mr. Jackson smiled. "I wanted to see how your wife was faring."

Mr. Francis shrugged. "Sick in the mornings. The doctor says that's normal.

"And I suppose you're rather busy here."

"About the same, tell you the truth. Some have quit, but we have fewer visitors these days. So I'm not getting any overtime."

"Sorry to hear that."

"Well, sir, I'd rather not anyway. I like the money, but it's better to get home to my wife."

"Good man. Listen, I'm still curious about that old lady. She never had anything to do with anyone here but you?"

His eyes widened. "Not that I recall. Strange, that you put it that way." He seemed to consider this. "Now that you mention it, I do remember once. It was one of the last times I saw her, I guess."

"What happened?"

"Well, she was here, talking like usual, and the dowager Duchess came up and greeted her! They talked like they were old friends. Then the Duchess says to me, 'We'll walk her home.' Then her husband comes up and off they go. Didn't think anything of it. I saw her again the very next day, and at least three or four more after that, too. Same time as always."

"And you never asked the Duchess about her? Where she lived?"

The young man paled. "I never thought to ask, sir."

"Busy as you are, with a wife and a child on the way, it's not surprising it slipped your mind. You mustn't blame yourself."

Lee stared at the desk. "Yes, sir." Then he raised his head. "What does it mean?"

Mr. Jackson thought about this. "It's not likely to mean anything. But I'll give them the sad news." He shook his head. "On top of everything else."

"How is the Duchess, sir?"

"She's as well as can be expected."

"Terrible shock. I hope they catch the man. Who would come into a hotel like this and attack an old woman?"

Mr. Jackson shook his head. "I honestly don't know."

When Mr. Jackson returned to his suite, he was pleased to discover his wife had ordered luncheon. She'd had it set up in her room.

"I thought you might be hungry after all that running about," she said.

While he was gone, Bessie had returned, and was now excitely running from him to her empty food bowl.

So he filled her bowl, and as the three of them ate, he told his wife about the old woman.

"How strange," she said. "The dowager knew this woman. And where she lived. Yet no one visited her for weeks?"

"Yes," he said. "I haven't told them yet, what with the attack and all. But it's very odd indeed."

"And she spoke of the poison tree. It sounds very much like the one you read about."

It did, and this bothered him, yet he didn't know why. He still had no proof that the tree in the conservatory here was the poison kind. "If this is the same tree, might Albert Stayman have told the old woman about it? The desk clerk said she'd been coming by with the same story for years. That would correspond with the time Albert and the Duchess have lived here."

Mrs. Jackson nodded slowly. "If they'd known each other in the past, perhaps so."

"But why come here every day, with the same story? And why never ask after her granddaughter? Or ask about her friends?"

"Old people do strange things. Perhaps she came here to see the girl, or the Duchess, then forgot. The only thing which impressed itself upon her mind was the tree."

He drank his coffee, not really thinking of anything. Then he rose. "Let me see if the Duchess is able to take visitors. She shouldn't hear of her friend's death from a desk clerk."

19

When Mr. Jackson went to the dowager's suite, Albert answered the door. "We're eating luncheon at present. Would you care to join us?"

Mr. Jackson stepped inside the room, speaking in a whisper. "How is she?"

Albert nodded. "Come see."

The dowager Duchess sat in their parlor at the table, looking much less pale. A bandage lay on her right temple. "Oh, my dear sir! Please, come join us."

Mr. Jackson went to her and knelt, kissing her hand. "My Lady, I'm pleased to see you improved."

She laughed. "Goodness me! No one's called me 'My Lady' in ages. Sit down! I insist. Have you eaten?"

"Just now." How could he possibly say this? "Unfortunately, I come with sad tidings."

Albert leaned forward. "What's happened?"

So Mr. Jackson told them about the old woman. "No one had any idea you knew her."

"Poor, poor Luella," the dowager said, wiping her eyes. "To end like that! Yes, I've known her since childhood. Her mother was a maid in our household. You might say we all grew up together."

Albert's face soured.

Cordelia glanced at him. "Now, Bertie, I know the two of you never got along, but —"

He nodded, not meeting anyone's gaze. "So how did you learn of all this?"

Mr. Jackson told them of the dog, and how it brought them to Luella's home. "So I suppose something good has come from this. My wife adores her little Bessie."

Cordelia said, "I remember the dog. She had it when we brought her home that once. She never let us in, which seemed unusual. But she was spry, and alert." She shook her head. "Such a pity."

"And you never went back to visit?"

The dowager's eyes widened. "Goodness, no! Not without an invitation. There are rules for the higher classes, sir." She smiled then. "Which you should well know."

Albert said, "She didn't seem ill at all. Although from what you say, she must've been."

At this, Cordelia rose. "Excuse me, sirs." She went to her room.

Albert said, "May I ask something personal?"

"Of course, sir. Anything."

A brief smile touched the old man's lips. "What did the sergeant mean, when he said you'd inserted yourself into the investigation?"

Why ask this? Mr. Jackson felt uneasy. "We've merely asked questions. The sergeant seems quite prickly when it comes to his case."

"I see. It just sounded odd to me. You're on your honeymoon, right?"

Mr. Jackson chuckled. "Of course we are! And I do say, enjoying ourselves, in spite of the difficulties. My wife's arm is improving, our room is splendid, and we're so happy to have found friends here." He studied Albert for his reaction.

But the man seemed distracted. "What? Oh, yes. Of course." He smiled back, but it never reached his eyes. "I feel honored to have you call me friend."

Cordelia returned, sat down, then peered at him. "Are you planning to grow a beard, Mr. Jackson?"

He laughed. "You're entirely correct, my Lady. I neglected to shave in my enthusiasm to trim trees with your husband this morning." He rose. "Perhaps I should visit the barber."

Cordelia grinned. "I'm only teasing." She held out her hand. "Must you go?"

"I should. Enjoy your luncheon."

He left, going back towards his rooms.

After letting his wife know he planned to visit the barbershop, there he went.

But the scene nagged at him. Something felt off about the whole exchange.

The barbershop had one other man in it, a portly fellow who wished his thick curly hair cut. A talkative one; while Mr. Jackson waited with a hot towel on his face, the man went on and on about the scene two nights earlier. "As soon as they called for a doctor, I knew the police would arrive. I knew it."

"Seems reasonable, sir," the barber said.

"Yes! I thought so too. But my wife wouldn't leave! Said it was her duty to stay, but I was sure she just wanted to see the scandal. Well, I said to her, I'm not staying here half the night just to see a scandal! I told her, if we don't go now, we'll be there until close to midnight. The very last thing I wanted was to be questioned by police. So I went out of the back way and to my room. She didn't get upstairs until close to midnight! She's still cross with me for saying it, but I told her so!"

Mr. Jackson held the towel on his face, moving it aside enough to say, "What back way?"

The man glanced over, eyes wide. "You didn't know? There's a back way from the dining hall! It's the same color as the walls, the handle too, so it's not very noticeable. But we got seated nearby the first time I came here. Goes right out to that hallway. You go right and the kitchens are just there! You can just walk right in. Of course, I wouldn't. Full of grease, and busy as all get-out. But you could go right in, if you wanted to. Not even a door!"

"Really," Mr. Jackson said.

"Yes, really! I was astonished the first time I saw it. Right into the kitchens! If you go left, it leads to the docks and all, but you can go round to your right after that and straight to the elevators." He gave a sharp nod, the barber jerking his scissors back in alarm. "You go that way, you don't have to push through the crowds after dinner. It's much faster to get to your room."

"Keep your head still, sir," the barber said, "and this will go much faster."

Mr. Jackson felt impressed. This answered a question he'd had all this time. "Thanks for the tip."

The man beamed. "My pleasure, sir. No trouble at all."

***

While Mr. Jackson was at the barbershop, Mrs. Jackson decided to look in on the dowager Duchess. Bringing Bessie with her, the two found the Duchess and her husband sitting in their parlor over the remains of luncheon.

"Come in, my dear," the dowager said.

The dowager's husband seemed less pleased, but said nothing, so Mrs. Jackson came in and sat at the table with them. "I hope you're well?"

"Oh, I'm just fine," she said. "I do wish they'd bring the old cook back." She pushed her plate away. "This new one's just not up to snuff."

Her husband rose. "Will you be here a while? I have something to do, and the doctor said she must be watched."

"I'd be happy to remain," Mrs. Jackson said with a smile. "You go about your business."

The dowager beamed. "I've ever so wanted to just sit and talk with you."

Mr. Stayman said, "I'll be back soon." He disappeared into his rooms.

When he said this, the dowager was in the midst of drinking her tea. "Yes, dear," she called out. "Hurry home."

The old lady turned to Mrs. Jackson. "How have you been?"

How had she been? "I'm well," she said, yet wasn't sure.

"Such enthusiasm!" The dowager patted Mrs. Jackson's hand, her tone somber. "I recall very well what it was like on our honeymoon. I loved Albert something terrible, I always have. But everything — a word, a kiss — reminded me of my first husband." She shook her head, glancing away, and Mrs. Jackson wondered if it would be the same way for her, four years from now. "You just want to do something, anything, to not remember," the dowager said, "yet, you never want to forget him either. It seems disloyal."

Mrs. Jackson nodded, eyes stinging. "Even being happy seems that way at times."

"Yes! Especially at first." The old dowager took Mrs. Jackson's hand in hers. "But you must focus on today, find a way to become ... I don't know. A new woman." She rubbed Mrs. Jackson's hand, then let go, sitting back. "Oh, it sounds all a foolishness —"

"No," Mrs. Jackson said, feeling hope for the first time and wanting to hear more. "Not at all."

The dowager smiled warmly. "I've been watching your young man. He's a good one."

"It's just ... we married so soon."

The dowager smiled to herself. "I had the same fears as you. Love can come to you in an instant, without warning. How long it stays is entirely up to you."

Mrs. Jackson nodded. It had happened that way before, and ended with so many regrets. "Death follows me wherever I go." She shook her head. "How can I allow this to go on?"

The dowager smiled to herself. "Do you love him?"

Mrs. Jackson peered at her hands. Did she? "It's complex."

The dowager chuckled softly. "As is all of life worth having." She took Mrs Jackson's hand in hers. "Dear girl, when you find someone who loves you, even for a moment, it's a gift! Seize it." She gave her a knowing smile. "Enjoy it. You don't know how long it'll last."

Could she possibly love this man, in the midst of such crushing grief? "I wish I knew how to proceed!"

"With kindness, my dear. Beginnings are such delicate times. Be kind to yourself and to him both. Teach yourself to trust him. And if you feel more warmly towards him, act on it at once," with this, she ground her fist into the palm of her hand, "crushing any harsh words before they emerge. It's all a matter of self-control."

Mrs. Jackson began to weep. "Oh, my dear husband! He loved me so very much. How I wish I'd been a better woman!" She lay her forehead on her crossed arms, pressing them to her knees as the tears flowed.

She sobbed for a long time, feeling the dowager's hand warm on her back. When the storm subsided, the old Duchess said, "Dear girl. We always wish we'd done better. But you can do better now, can you not? You have a second chance. Take it."

***

After his shave, Mr. Jackson headed to his suite. One of the bellboys stood waiting for the elevator. "I hope the funeral went well."

The young man nodded.

"I'm sorry for your loss," Mr. Jackson said.

"Thank you," the man said.

They stood waiting in silence.

"What sort of flowers did Mr. Stayman bring?"

The young man blinked. "Bring? I have no idea." Then he frowned. "I don't actually recall seeing him there."

Odd. "I heard he planned to attend."

The bellboy shrugged. "I suppose. He did dote on Miss Agnes — had her do all his errands for him. Paid her well, too. She'd always pay for a round when we went down to the —"

His face went pale, and he pressed his gloved hands to his mouth.

Mr. Jackson smiled to himself. "No need to fret. We all deserve a night out once in a while."

The young man's cheeks reddened. "Thank you, sir."

The elevators opened, and Mr. Jackson returned to his suite, where his wife handed him a message. "We're invited for dinner again."

He chuckled. "I suppose we must have made a good enough impression."

"But we were just there last night! I wonder what he wants."

This seemed a fair question. "Perhaps he's gotten some new information he wishes to share with us."

"Oh," Mrs. Jackson said. "A package came for you as well. I had them put it in your room."

"Now what might that be?"

On his dresser sat a large flat rectangular brown paper parcel an inch thick tied with twine. On opening it, he exclaimed, "Would you look at that!"

Mrs. Jackson hurried in. "Are you well?"

He opened the note inside:

Contacted every library in the area. Schaumburg had it. —Nestor

He held the book up. "It's the one! The book I wanted."

Her face grew pale. "The one you went to see the librarian for?"

"Why, yes."

His wife's face turned alarmed. "You must let no one know you have it. This is too much of a coincidence."

Could the librarian have been killed to stop him from reading a book about a tree? It seemed quite unlikely. "Then I shall read it at once."

And so he did. The book was old, with large print and margins. It went into great detail, mostly about the tree's various medicinal and poisonous characteristics. He did, however, find a section on the tree itself. Much of it was how to grow the thing, but then he found an illustration!

"This is it," he murmured, feeling excited. This was the tree in the hotel's garden! He turned the page, which had a drawing of a man's hand holding one of the seeds. The seed was almost the size of a quarter, but thicker. Something about it seemed familiar.

His wife walked in. "Find anything?"

"I don't know," he said.

"Is it the same tree as in the garden downstairs?"

"Most definitely," he said. "But there's something else ... "

She sat beside him. "What?"

"I don't know." He shook his head. "It'll come to me." He smiled at her, patted her knee. "It always does." He put the book underneath the bed, up in the springs so no one might stumble across it. "Now, where would you like to go for tea?"

***

As his wife needed her medication, they decided to stay in their rooms for tea, visiting Mr and Mrs. Carlo for dinner.

After dinner, the couples moved to the parlor. Mr and Mrs. Carlo had alcohol, Mrs. Jackson had tea, and Mr. Jackson, coffee. For a few minutes they drank silently, then Mr. Carlo rose. "Might I have a word in private, sir?"

Mr and Mrs. Jackson glanced at each other. "Very well," Mr. Jackson said. He leaned over. "Let me see what this is about," he whispered, then kissed her cheek and followed Mr. Carlo to his study.

The room was paneled in oak, stained a dark golden brown. The fixtures, brass. The lampshades, white frosted glass. Mr. Carlo moved behind his desk, but didn't sit. "How's the investigation coming?"

"Difficult to say. As yet we have much information, yet little idea as to how to proceed."

"We?"

"Well, yes. My wife has been helpful, and I believe the sergeant on the case is becoming amenable to our help as well."

Mr. Carlo gave a tiny snort of amusement. "Then you perhaps may not want him to see this." He pulled out a large sheet of white paper.

Upon it sat the words "Wanted For Questioning."

It also had a photo of Mr. Jackson's wife.

20

Mr. Jackson's mind went utterly blank.

Mr. Carlo said, "My people control Chicago Station. Nothing gets shipped in or out — at least not that way — without going through me. So imagine my surprise when sixty cases of this flier arrived today!"

Mr. Jackson stared at Mr. Carlo in horror.

"A woman wanted for questioning by the Feds in connection with several high-profile murders checks into my hotel, and people begin to die. A coincidence? I don't believe in them." He smiled, but it was unpleasant. "I don't like my hotel being sullied in this manner. So you have a choice. You stop this madwoman — whoever she might be — or my sixty cases of fliers find their way to your sergeant's desk."

Mr. Jackson peered at the man: a most dangerous snake indeed. "What's to stop you from sending them to him anyway?"

Mr. Carlo chuckled. "Nothing so crass. We're gentlemen here!" His lip curled in disdain. "Prolonged blackmail is a most unpleasant business."

Yet short-term blackmail didn't seem to be beneath the man. "You know, I've told the sergeant everything — except about the speakeasy beneath your soda bar."

Mr. Carlo's eyes narrowed. Then burst into laughter. "You think I'm afraid of that? At most, we'd get a week's shutdown and a bit of publicity. But all publicity is good, and that kind is even better!"

For an instant, Mr. Jackson felt dismayed. Then it came to him: his wife had been right. He held out his hand. "You have a deal." The two men shook hands. "And I'll take that flier."

"What could you possibly want that for?"

Mr. Jackson didn't move or speak. Finally, Mr. Carlo handed it over.

Mr. Jackson folded the flier into quarters. "What I want this for is my concern." He slid the flier into his jacket pocket. "I'll find your killer. But I'll also do whatever it takes to protect my interests."

Mr. Carlo gave him an amused smile. "As I will to protect mine."

***

Mrs. Jackson and Maisy Carlo had spent the time Mr. Jackson was gone engaged in small talk. Mrs. Jackson heartily disliked small talk, so when Mr. Jackson returned from his meeting with Mr. Carlo, at first she was glad.

But one look at him told a different story: Mr. Jackson seemed uneasy, quiet. As the couple got into Mr. Carlo's car to return to the hotel, Mrs. Jackson asked, "What was all that about?"

Mr. Jackson's eyes flickered to the driver. "Perhaps we can discuss this another time?"

She nodded. The driver surely reported what was said here to his employer. Yet what might Mr. Carlo have wanted to speak to Mr. Jackson about which she couldn't be party to?

When they got to their suite, Mr. Jackson immediately left for his room, leaving her to stand in the parlor. It sounded as if he was telephoning someone.

The whole situation unnerved her, and the longer she stood there, the more uneasy she became. Whatever was going on?

The door opened and Mr. Jackson emerged. "Come, sit."

"What's going on?"

"Please, my dear, sit down."

So they sat at the big round table.

Mr. Jackson said, "You asked about the meeting I had with Mr. Carlo." He presented a "Wanted" flier with her portrait on it.

She stared at it in terror. "I knew it!" She rushed to her room.

Mr. Jackson followed her. "What are you doing?"

She began taking her clothes from the closet. "We have to get out of here!"

"Nonsense. This is the least of our worries."

She tossed a dress on her bed. "I don't understand. What are we going to do?"

"I'll take care of everything." He rested his hands on her shoulders. "Tomorrow, I'll visit the sergeant, and —"

"And what?"

"Show this to him."

He planned to betray her? She began to cry, throwing his hands off her. "What? No! I trusted you!"

Mr. Jackson's voice was filled with compassion. "Come here."

For an instant, she hesitated. Had her worst rival trapped her in this marriage only to betray her? But then, the dowager's words came to her: *he's a good man ... teach yourself to trust him.*

With an effort, she let him take her into his arms, hold her. And her mind began to work once more. He wouldn't betray her: he'd made his vow. He seemed to care about her.

But she couldn't stop crying. When they finally thought they were safe, everything was falling apart.

And she had a sudden fear: had she doomed him as well?

"Oh, my dear girl. I'm sorry to frighten you so," he said, smoothing her hair. "But don't you see? Of all the perils we face, Mr. Carlo is the most dangerous. If we don't pull his fangs, he'll hold that flier over us forever."

"But what if we're arrested?"

He kissed her forehead, then drew back, gazing at her, his hands holding her face. "My dear girl. No one's going to arrest us."

"But why?"

He grinned. "I know who the killer is."

Astonishment, and hope. "Oh ..."

"They need us. All will be well, you'll see." He chuckled fondly, smoothed wet curls back from her face. "I will never let anyone harm you. You have my word. Here's what we'll do ..."

21

To Mr. Jackson's delight, the newspaper headline read:

LIBRARIAN MURDERED

Poisoner Strikes Again

He made a short phone call to an old friend, then headed on his way.

When Mr. Jackson arrived at the police station, reporters had camped out in the parking lot. The station itself swarmed with people. He had to push through the crowd to get to the front desk, but was brought into the sergeant's office at once.

Sergeant Nestor put his newspaper down, and took his feet off his open lower desk drawer. "What can I do for you?"

Mr. Jackson tossed his newspaper onto the sergeant's desk.

"Yeah," the sergeant said. "I got a call at 6 A.M. from the Chief of Police." He rubbed his eyes and yawned.

"Whoever thought putting telephones in houses was a good idea —"

"How's the investigation going?"

The sergeant shook his head. "I have no leads, and the situation is getting stickier by the minute."

Mr. Jackson leaned a hand on the sergeant's desk. "**Now** would you like my help?"

"That depends. What sort of help are we talking about?"

"I know who the killer is."

Sergeant Nestor jumped to his feet. "Close the door."

When Mr. Jackson did so, the sergeant said, "How do you know?"

"At this point I have no tangible proof." Mr. Jackson shrugged. "Just a very good hunch. And my observations, of course."

The sergeant let out a breath. "So you don't know." He turned away, sat down. "Okay. Tell me about your hunch."

Mr. Jackson sat. "First, I need your help."

"Sure," the sergeant said. "What's wrong?"

Mr. Jackson took out the flier.

Sergeant Nestor's eyes widened. He glanced up at Mr. Jackson. "Is this real? Is she involved in all this?"

"This came to my attention last night. I thought bringing this to you would be the best course of action, since you wanted to know everything."

"This explains the evasions." The sergeant put his elbows on his desk. "How exactly did this come to your attention?"

That was an item Mr. Jackson hoped could be held back for later. He hesitated, wondering what to reveal.

Sergeant Nestor peered at him. "You're braver than I thought. Who's blackmailing you?"

So he saw right through it. "Carlo," Mr. Jackson said. "He has sixty cases of them." But they still had a play. "If you'll help us, I'll tell you everything."

Sergeant Nestor's eyes narrowed, but his voice was surprisingly kind. "What's going on, son?"

Mr. Jackson took a deep breath, let it out. Perhaps this would work after all. "Neither of us ever wanted to be involved with the Mob," he gestured at the flier, "back home. But we got caught up in it. We're trying to get out. There was an ambush, and my wife was injured. She lost her husband and her son in one night. But she found a surgeon who would treat her. We met up at the station." He smiled to himself. "Got married on the ship," he glanced at the sergeant. "I wanted to make life easier for her."

Sergeant Nestor nodded.

"But they have Feds on their payroll. Don't you see? This," he pointed at the flier, "they're using them to find us."

"So you want protection."

"Yes."

"You want me to impede a Federal investigation."

"Well, if you put it that way, yes."

"And in return, you'll help me with **this** investigation."

"Free of charge. Just keep us out of it."

Sergeant Nestor glanced aside, then back. "Why does this feel like you just played me?"

Mr. Jackson made his face all innocence. "Whatever do you mean?"

"If I turn you in and you're telling the truth, you'll be killed. I'd have that on my conscience forever. But even if this entire story is a fabrication — which I suspect it is — I can't get your help if you're shipped out of the city." He glared at the flier. "The two of you will disappear into Federal custody. If there's a plea agreement having anything to do with this matter, it'll come weeks from now, if ever. Who knows how many will be poisoned in that time?"

"Then it's settled." Mr. Jackson held out his hand. "I'll take that back, if you please."

"Most certainly not!"

"It's not worth anything to you, and my wife would feel ever so much better if she knew I had it."

"Why would I ever give it back?"

"Because if you don't, I walk out of here."

"Not if I arrest you for obstruction."

"Sergeant Nestor, I'm not obstructing anything. I came here voluntarily, to help." He shook his head mournfully, letting his shoulders droop. "Such a pity. You could have been a hero! But even though I came to you with the name of the killer, risking my life to do so, you turned me down. If you arrest me, my lawyers will stand up, right in the middle of the press conference your Chief of Police is planning out front, and share the entire sordid tale. Imagine his reaction to **that**! He'd have to at least censure you, just from the embarrassment alone."

The sergeant paled. "You wouldn't dare!"

Mr. Jackson chuckled. "I dare quite a lot these days. Makes life exhilarating." He checked his watch. "My lawyers should be here by now. Should I send them off, or invite them in?"

Sergeant Nestor's eyes narrowed. "What's the name?"

"Name, sir?"

"Of your lawyer?"

"Whoever they sent from River, Heater, and Rock."

Sergeant Nestor pressed a button on his desk, and a blast of crowd noise came forth. "Allen?"

Silence, then in the cacophony came: "Yes, sergeant?"

"Is anyone out there from River, Heater, and Rock?"

A silence, then, "Looks like all three of them, sir."

"What color are they?"

"White, sir, all three."

Sergeant Nestor gave a weary sigh. He punched the button. "Send them home."

"Sir?"

"Tell them Mr. Jackson won't be needing their services today." He let go of the button, handed over the flier. "One day, you're going to tell me what that's really about."

Mr. Jackson looked the man straight in the eye. "She didn't kill anyone."

"So you say."

Mr. Jackson smiled. He had him.

"Very well," the sergeant finally said. "But if it gets out that I made this deal with you, the last thing I do before I'm sent to Federal prison is to drag you two there myself."

"I would expect nothing less," Mr. Jackson said. "Now let's discuss how to lure our culprit into the open."

22

The next day, Mr. Montgomery Carlo, the prestigious owner of the recently beleaguered Myriad Hotel, made an announcement. Due to the recent troubles, he proposed "sweeping changes" to the establishment. To prepare for this, he planned to take a tour of the Hotel the next day, examining every area of it to see what might be eliminated.

The staff was abuzz with the news. What did it mean?

Some hoped it meant their widely disliked manager would be fired. Others worried their own jobs were in danger.

At dinner, Albert Stayman was furious. "Sweeping changes? What does the pompous fool mean by that?"

"Now, Bertie," his wife Cordelia said. "Monty means well."

"I wouldn't put it past him to take out my gardens, just to spite me."

"Well," Mr. Jackson said. "I don't know if you knew, but he and his wife invited us to dinner the other day. He did mention something about the gardens. Just in passing, of course."

Albert's face darkened. "You see?"

Mrs. Jackson said brightly, "Who knows? Perhaps he wants to expand them."

"But where? Would he move them? Some of those plants don't do well with moving."

As if on cue, a desk clerk came up to Albert with a note.

Cordelia said, "What is it, Bertie?"

"He wants to meet with us both tomorrow, by my tree at noon," Albert said. "About 'the future of the gardens'."

"I wonder what that means," Mr. Jackson said.

"I'm sure it'll be fine." Cordelia put her hand on his and said firmly, "I'll make sure no harm comes to your gardens — I promise you that."

Albert abruptly rose. "I need some air." He hurried off, leaving the entire table staring after him.

"Talk of change always upsets him," Cordelia said. "He'll be fine."

Mr. Jackson rose. "Let me see to him."

Following out to the lobby, he glimpsed Albert moving towards the front doors from the direction of the front desk. He hurried across the wide lobby and through the doors. Albert turned left and rushed up the street.

"Mr. Stayman!"

Albert glanced back but didn't stop.

Mr. Jackson ran to catch him. "Mr. Stayman, please."

Albert snapped, "What do you want?"

"What's wrong? What troubles you so?"

"What troubles me, young man, is that the shop I wish to visit closes at nine, and the clock just struck half past eight. So if you'll excuse me?" He hurried off, leaving Mr. Jackson gaping after him.

What could the man possibly need to purchase in such a hurry? The front desk could order anything needed immediately, or he could wait to order it tomorrow.

Shaking his head, Mr. Jackson returned to his dinner, which had gone cold.

***

The next day dawned stormy. Thunder boomed, rain beat against the windows. Mrs. Jackson turned from the balcony, closed the glass doors. "Do you think your plan will work with all this noise?

Mr. Jackson held up the paper. "The storm will pass before breakfast. One thing they say here: Don't like the weather? Wait an hour."

She grinned at him, amused.

Their servants arrived, and Mrs. Jackson went for her bath. "Your arm is looking much better today," Mrs. Knight said. "How does it feel?"

"Improved," Mrs. Jackson said. The pain was improved, true, but the arm didn't wish to entirely straighten.

But she didn't despair. After all, the doctor said that her arm hadn't been sewn correctly — perhaps the specialist would be able to help.

Mr. Jackson had been right: by the time she came out of her bath, the storm had passed. After Mrs. Knight fixed her hair, Mrs. Jackson felt chilly, and went to fetch her shawl. When she lifted the shawl from the dresser drawer, her holster sat empty.

She stared at the empty holster, shocked. Where was her gun?

"Is something wrong, ma'am?"

Her mind raced. Her heart pounded. "Have you spoken to anyone about my gun?"

Mrs. Knight came up beside her. "No, ma'am — oh, good gracious!"

Mrs. Jackson closed the drawer. "This is bad." She looked at the maid, who'd gone pale. "Please call your next client and let them know you'll have to cancel."

"Cancel, ma'am?"

"The police will wish to speak with you."

23

Sergeant Nestor was not happy. "Why did you have a gun here in the first place?"

She'd never noticed how dark the carpet was until now. "It was a gift from a friend. I don't even have bullets for it. I had need of it when I was a private investigator, but now ... I keep it for sentimental reasons."

The sergeant squinted at her for a moment in a frowning sort of way, then pointed to the open drawer. "Yet here sits a well-used calf holster."

She shrugged. "It seemed the best way to carry it."

"Who knew it was here?"

"Mrs. Knight," she frowned, trying to recall. "That's all."

Mr. Jackson stood a few paces away, hand to his chin. "I never knew she had it with her. Although I should have guessed."

The sergeant let out a breath. "If it sat in your drawer, half the maids in the hotel knew it was there."

He shook his head. "The hotel has a safe in it for a reason." He turned to Mrs. Knight. "You can go."

Mrs. Knight looked devastated, and Mrs. Jackson felt compassion on her. "I'll see you at seven tonight, then?"

The color returned to the woman's face. "Yes, of course, ma'am."

Once she'd left, Sergeant Nestor said, "When did you last see it?"

"Several days past," Mrs. Jackson said. "The first day we arrived. I put my shawl atop the holster, and I haven't needed either until now."

The sergeant turned to Mr. Jackson. "Now there's a good chance our culprit is armed. Are you sure you want to continue with your plan?"

"I do," he said.

Mrs. Jackson thought it best to say nothing.

The sergeant looked at her, then at Mr. Jackson. "Well, I suppose we best start questioning the staff."

24

At breakfast, the dowager Duchess seemed even less amused than the sergeant. Her husband looked a wreck. Circles lay dark under his eyes, and the old man's hands shook so that he could hardly keep his food upon his fork.

Mrs. Jackson said, "I hope you're well, sir."

The old man gave her a level look. "Thank you. I only wish this day to end. And it will, one way or another."

His wife patted his hand. "All will be well, my dear, never you fret."

Mrs. Jackson said, "All days end, sir. I hope that today yours becomes more pleasant."

To her surprise, the old man's eyes reddened. "Such a sweet girl you are."

"Why, thank you, sir."

***

As they left the dining hall, the lobby was in a commotion. Preparations were being made for the owner's tour, and reporters had begun to arrive.

The couple went for a stroll in the park after breakfast, discussing their plans. As Mr. Jackson had predicted, the day was now sunny, if cool.

Mrs. Jackson said, "Are you certain this will work?"

Mr. Jackson shrugged. "The sergeant seemed to believe so."

"But what if our culprit is armed?"

"It's unlikely the same person took your gun." But although Mr. Jackson intentionally made his words sound convincing, he wasn't so sure. "Even so, do you really think this will end in violence?"

Mrs. Jackson nodded. "It is unlikely."

He hoped for all their sakes that this was true.

The couple returned to the hotel as the clock struck noon.

"I could fancy a stroll in the garden right now," Mr. Jackson said. He turned to his wife. "My dear, let's give the Duchess and her husband some moral support. Albert in particular may have need of us."

The garden was empty but for the fish in the pond, a bird here and there, and at the back by the snake-wood tree, Albert and Cordelia. A freshly-turned patch of dirt lay near the tree, neatly tamped down.

Cordelia sat on a bench. Albert paced, wringing his hands. He stopped to stare at the couple when they moved into view. "What are you doing here?"

"Now, Bertie —" Cordelia said.

"We just fancied a stroll," Mr. Jackson said. "And we wanted to offer our support. I hope you're well?"

Albert let his hands drop to his sides. "How did it ever come to this?"

"Let's sit down," Mr. Jackson said. "We'll wait here with you."

Albert sat beside Cordelia. Mrs. Jackson sat next to her, while Mr. Jackson sat beside Albert.

A slight movement ruffled trees in the distance.

Mr. Jackson said, "You've been upset many a day, sir. As your friend, I'd like to help." He glanced at his wife, who nodded. "We both would. Please, tell us what's wrong."

"How can I?" Albert put his face in his hands.

"Well, then," Mrs. Jackson said. "I suppose we'll have to share what we've observed." She gazed down, hesitant. "But we have a confession to make."

This captured their attention at once. Cordelia said, "Confession, dear?"

"Indeed," Mr. Jackson said. "You were right," he said to Albert. "We are on our honeymoon." He grinned at his wife. "But I wasn't entirely honest with you on another matter."

Albert seemed subdued. "What matter is that?"

Mr. Jackson took a deep breath, let it out. "Before we came here, we've both worked as private investigators —"

"Oh," Cordelia said, impressed.

"- and we've been helping the police find this killer."

"Oh," Albert said, dismayed. "Somehow, I knew it!"

Mrs. Jackson turned to Cordelia. "My dear Lady, I must ask: why did you do it?"

Cordelia blinked. "Do what?"

"Kill all those people."

Albert's face turned outraged. "What?"

Cordelia laughed. "I could never —"

Stern-faced policemen moved out from behind the trees, hands on their holstered guns. Sergeant Nestor was with them.

Cordelia looked horrified. "Why — how?"

"I'm sorry, My Lady," Mr. Jackson said. "I truly am. But if you promise to go quietly, they won't have to use the handcuffs."

Albert said, "No!" His eyes turned red. "You can't be serious. Not Cordelia! She didn't do it!"

Sergeant Nestor said, "Then who did?"

Albert peered at his hands. "It was me."

25

The dowager Duchess looked as shocked as her husband had moments before. "But Bertie, why?"

Sergeant Nestor took out a notepad and pencil. "Sir, let's start from the beginning."

"Very well," Albert said, still peering at his hands. "But you must believe me: I didn't kill the clerk."

"I know," Sergeant Nestor said. "I've just heard from the coroner: it was entirely natural. An aneurysm burst in his brain. Poor fellow died at once."

"I suppose that's a relief," Albert said. "But him dying got me thinking it was a good time to begin."

"Begin?" Sergeant Nestor seemed confused.

"Yes! I hated that fool manager, always sneering at us, calling us 'tenants'. Like my darling Cordelia was a servant! And once he even called me a four-flusher! As if I was only with my wife for her money. The very idea! So I sent Agnes with the sauce for the manager's cake." At that, his face crumpled, his eyes reddening. "But I told her — I **told** her not to eat it! She must have tasted it anyway." Tears stood in his eyes. "Oh, the poor girl!"

"Why do you care so much?" The sergeant put his foot up on a rock. "Who's Agnes to you?"

"Oh, Bertie," Cordelia said, horrified realization dawning in her face. "No."

But Albert seemed not to hear her. "Cordelia always tried to match us, me and Luella. She never thought it worked. But we were mad for each other, though we could never stand being in the same room for more than an hour." He shook his head. "It makes no sense, when you say it that way."

Mrs. Jackson said, "What happened?"

He gave out a self-mocking snort. "What usually happens. She came with child and was dismissed. She moved away. It was either that or marry me, I suppose, and we both knew that would have been a disaster."

Sergeant Nestor said, "When did you learn Agnes was here?"

"Soon after we moved here," Albert said. "Her mother — our daughter, I suppose — had passed away. I knew that, but I never knew of Agnes until I saw her. I knew her when I saw her, though: she looked just like Luella did when she was young." He shook his head. "Luella had the poor girl almost a slave. I went to call on her and Agnes was out front, beaten up and scared. I

215

took her out to eat and she told me of it all. I told Agnes come with me, I'll get you some place better."

"So that's how she got the job here," the sergeant said.

Albert nodded. "I never told her who I was, and Luella never saw me. But I think she must have heard Agnes was here, because she showed up a few weeks back."

"Now that's odd," Mr. Jackson said, "because the desk clerk said she came often, and spoke of your tree."

"Oh! I remember," Albert said. "I'd written Luella about the tree when we went to India, before we moved here. She always loved plants; it was the only thing we had in common."

The whole time, Cordelia had been staring at Albert, mouth open. "Agnes was your granddaughter?" The dowager Duchess seemed appalled. "Oh, my poor Bertie." She wrapped her arms around him.

The rustle of the waterfall was all one might hear, at least for a while. Finally, Sergeant Nestor said, "And the waiter?"

"I didn't know Agnes was dead," Albert moaned. "But when the manager didn't die, I thought I'd done something wrong. Not put enough in. I heard the owner would be staying here, and —"

"You put poison in his lemon-cake," Mrs. Jackson said.

Albert nodded.

Mr. Jackson said, "But why kill the librarian? He'd done nothing to you."

"You saw my seeds! And my drill! I couldn't let you get the book, too — once you saw the drawing of the seeds, you'd have known everything."

Sergeant Nestor said, "The seeds and the drill was for —"

"It's how I got the poison," Albert said mournfully.

"Bertie," Cordelia said, horrified. "Was it you that knocked me down?"

"I'm so sorry," Albert moaned. "But I had to get everything out! And I couldn't let you see me in there — you thought I was at her funeral. I didn't mean it." He took her hands. "I'd never do anything to harm you, not on purpose."

"I know," she said.

"So you took advantage of the desk clerk's natural death to kill the manager, and on failing to kill him, you tried to kill the owner," Mr. Jackson said. "And when you thought I might learn the truth, you killed the librarian as well, to keep me from it."

"Yes," Albert said.

Mrs. Jackson said, "But why?"

"Yes," Sergeant Nestor said. "You said the manager sneered at you. But the owner lets you live here free of charge. By all accounts from the staff, you've seemed happy. Why try to kill him?"

"I spent my life tending the Duke's estate. His gardens. Once he died, though, we had to sell the properties to afford a funeral fit for a Duke. I couldn't help her, not really. She was in such a state. And I knew nothing about such matters." Albert's head drooped. "All that — the mansion, the gardens — everything I'd worked for my entire life, gone."

"Surely the new owners enjoy your work," Mr. Jackson said.

"Carlo bought the estate." Albert shook his head. "Claimed all would be cared for. But not ten minutes after my wife signed the papers, he told us he'd changed his mind. He planned to turn it into another of his hotels. My poor plants! He ripped out my entire flower garden to put in," at this, he faltered, "tennis courts!"

The sergeant looked up from his notepad. "Was it then you decided to kill him?"

"Yes, but only with the vaguest of idea as to how, until I saw the seeds in a shop and learned of their properties."

Mr. Jackson said, "But why not just kill him **then**? Why wait until now?"

"We had nothing." He shook his head, spoke with fierce anger. "We were sent packing like tramps. My wife wept so bitterly when we left that day. And on that day, I made my plan: I wanted Montgomery Carlo ruined, utterly ruined. I wanted him disgraced. I wanted him to fall into scandal and bankruptcy, to lose everything he had, just as she did. I wanted everything taken from him, just as he'd taken everything from her."

The dowager had sat quietly, sadness in her eyes. "Oh, Bertie. That day, I wept for my husband. I wept for the memories there. Not for the house. Not even for the properties or the money or any of it."

He looked appalled at this. "Was I not good enough for you, then?"

"I have always loved you. Yet I also loved him. I still had to grieve."

"But I did it for **you**!" Tears stood in his ancient eyes. "And when the value of the hotel declined, I had enough saved to buy it for you! So you might have property again. Be respected. Have an income."

She clasped his face in her hands. "Whatever would I do with a hotel, Bertie? How would I manage it? I know nothing of such things." She let her hands fall to his shoulders. "And now we're to be separated yet again, after all we've been through."

"I know," he said. "I'm so sorry."

Sergeant Nestor closed his notebook and went to Albert, who stood. "Albert Stayman, you're under arrest for murder." The sergeant patted Albert down, taking something from the old man's jacket pocket. "Your gun, ma'am," he said to Mrs. Jackson, and handed it over.

Cordelia stared at her husband, appalled.

Mrs. Jackson — much relieved — put the gun in her pocket. "How did you know it was in my room?"

"I overheard the maids talking." He shrugged, head drooping. "I'm sorry I stole it." Albert sounded defeated. "I think I went a bit mad at the idea of Monty ruining the garden here — I thought I'd kill him at last." He looked around. "He's not coming, is he?"

The sergeant handed Albert off to a couple of uniformed men. "No, he never was."

The policemen brought Albert a few yards away, and his wife followed. Mr. Jackson pointed to the freshly turned patch of dirt by the snake-wood tree. "I believe you'll find all the things Mr. Stayman took from their rooms there."

Albert's face fell.

Sergeant Nestor gestured to his men, who began digging. He turned to Mr. Jackson, and asked quietly. "How did you know he'd talk?"

"He wouldn't, if you questioned him directly. But I knew he'd talk when we accused his wife." Mr. Jackson smiled at the old couple. "He might love her even more than his gardens." He went to Albert, then turned to the officer. "Might I speak with him in private for just a moment?"

The officer glanced at Sergeant Nestor, who nodded. Cordelia and the officer moved a few paces away.

Mr. Jackson said quietly, "Mr. Stayman, there's something which still troubles me."

Albert raised red eyes to him. "What?"

"What really happened to Miss Luella?"

He nodded, glancing away. "After what she did to Agnes, I was convinced she'd gone completely mad. I told Helen I wanted to make a friend cookies, and she let me into the shop one night." At that, he faltered. "I sent Luella cookies made with the crumbled hard bits of one of the seeds." He shook his head. "I thought it'd kill her, and my little Agnes would be free. When I spoke with the desk clerk just now, and he told me how she was ... and I realized what I'd done to her —" Tears filled his eyes. "Three years, she lived that way." His head hung low. "I've made a complete mess of everything. I regret it all, every bit."

Mr. Jackson put his hand on the old man's shoulder. "Thank you for telling me the truth. I think you'll feel much better now." He stepped back, let the officer take hold of Albert's arm again.

Sergeant Nestor came up to him. "What was that about?"

Mr. Jackson said, "The truth. I think he's truly sorry for what he's done."

Sergeant Nestor shrugged. "I just catch 'em. What happens next is in the court's hands."

A cloth bag came free of the dirt below the snake-wood tree. When opened, it held the library book, its record card, the mortar and pestle, the hand drill, and the bookmark-sized strip of red cloth with three poison seeds attached.

Sergeant Nestor stared at the bag, then at Mr. Jackson, blinking in astonishment. "How did you —?"

Mr. Jackson shrugged. "Another hunch. But it seemed reasonable."

Albert turned to Mr. Jackson. "Take care of Cordelia, will you? And make sure she has flowers."

Mr. Jackson smiled at him. "I'd be honored."

They led Albert Stayman off, the dowager Duchess trailing behind.

Mr. Jackson put an arm around his wife's shoulders. "The things we do for love."

26

The couple stayed at the hotel — all expenses paid, of course — until all the questions and searches ended and they were declared free to go. It was nice to be able to relax without the worry of catching a killer.

They went to a posh little cinema near Grant Park to see their talkie, and Mrs. Jackson thought that the sight and sounds of it were just as astonishing as Mr. Jackson had described. Afterward, the two strolled along the boardwalk, a magnificent view of the lake before them, their little dog Bessie running back and forth alongside.

Mr. Jackson said, "Do you find this marriage agreeable so far?"

Mrs. Jackson pondered this a moment, then smiled up at him. "I do!"

He appeared pleased with himself. "And how do you find our accommodations?"

She shrugged. "Beautiful, sumptuous. Nothing a murder here and there can't undo."

At this, Mr. Jackson chuckled. "My dear, I find you most amusing."

"An 'entertaining companion', as you once put it," she said, also amused. Then she considered recent events. "You're quite perceptive. A masterful job discovering the man behind all these murders. And the stolen items!" She felt humbled. "Perhaps a better investigator than I."

"I'm quite honored. Then shall we remain here in Chicago for a while? At this Myriad Hotel?"

"I don't see why not," Mrs. Jackson said.

They continued to stroll along.

Mr. Jackson said, "How do you feel?"

She considered this most seriously. "I feel good. I feel well." She moved her injured arm in its sling. "It doesn't pain me." *You must find a way to become a new woman.* She stopped, took the sling off, then tossed it into the lake, where it floated, sank. "I feel free."

Mr. Jackson chuckled. "You know, you might need that again, after we consult the specialist."

She shrugged. "I'm sure the doctor will have another one if I do."

"Well, now that you're well, I intend to give you a proper honeymoon." He gestured with enthusiasm as he spoke. "We'll dance at the nightclubs, sail the lake —"

Amused by the mention of sailing, she turned to face him, looking into his dark eyes. Then she took his hands, interlacing his dark brown fingers in hers. "Have you ever been with a woman?"

He didn't flinch, nor glance away, but to her surprise, he blushed. "I have not. Men have always been my downfall." He smiled shyly, still gazing into her eyes. "But I'd be willing to make an exception with you."

She smiled. "Ah, yes. For the sight of my legs."

"For the sight of your legs. They ... are ... stunning."

"On one condition."

"I'll do anything you ask."

"Kiss me."

"Here? In public?"

"No one will care." She gave him a wry smile. "Besides, I don't show my legs to just anyone."

"Ever the investigator, are we? Well, then," he said, moving closer, "I —"

Looking into his dark eyes reminded her so poignantly of another kiss, the dark eyes of another man now dead, that her vision blurred. "I —"

"Let me love you," he said softly. "I know it's much too soon to expect your love in return. But can you forget the griefs of the past and your fears for the future, and just for this one instant, be happy?"

It was too much, too close to what that man she'd loved so very much had said the day he died. And she couldn't help herself, couldn't stop herself, couldn't hide from the reality in front of her, not anymore. *You have a second chance. Take it.*

"I can," she said, and kissed her new husband with all her heart.

As it turned out, he was a very good kisser.

Some time later, she took his arm, as seagulls flew high across the lake in the sunshine. "I think it's time we began our proper honeymoon."

Epilogue

Albert Stayman was convicted of the librarian's murder. He was also convicted of the attempted murders of manager Flannery Davis and hotel owner Montgomery Carlo, which led to the negligent poisonings of Agnes Odds and George Neuberg. Mr. Jackson arranged to have Albert transferred to a prison which had a garden.

Mr. Carlo was charged with blackmail, but charges were dropped after Sergeant Nestor watched sixty cases of fliers go into an incinerator.

Duchess Cordelia Stayman continued to live at the Myriad Hotel, and true to Mr. Jackson's word, was kept well-supplied with flowers.

George Neuberg recovered from his poisoning, and returned to being a waiter at the Myriad Hotel. The couple spent many a happy weekend thereafter, sailing the lake with George and his family.

Mr. Lee Francis was promoted to head desk clerk, a title which came with a raise. He and his wife were blessed with a son several months later.

Eugene and Helen were married, and while Eugene still did much of the "dirty work," the hotel hired an outside service to take care of the rats.

After the manager failed to find a Cook who would agree to join the Hotel, the couple recommended a young Chef of their acquaintance — a recent graduate from the Cordon Bleu — who was most happy for the opportunity.

The snake-wood tree was donated to a conservatory specializing in poison plants, where it lived happily thereafter, visitors from around the world marveling at its story.

After an outpouring of sympathy, a settlement from Mr. Carlo, and the encouragement of the couple, Miss Goldie Jean Dab opened a shop of her own. Its sign read:

THE EXONERATED COOK

Dishes To Die For!

It became the most popular bistro in town.

The Vanishing Valet!

Coming soon!

To learn more about the Myriad Mysteries,

join Claire Logan's Facebook page.

Acknowledgements

Thanks so much to Melissa Williams for beta reading for me, and to Patricia Loofbourrow for the cover design. I appreciate it so much!

About the Author

I've loved reading since I can remember! I love puzzles and mysteries and intrigue, and of all the cities I've been to, Chicago is my favorite. My four years living in Chicago during grad school were wonderful. Plus I love history. And wasn't the 1920's wild? I've always wanted to write a series set in Chicago and now here's my chance.

Made in the USA
Coppell, TX
26 November 2020

42119751R10136